Whisper of the Rock Elephant

(Ashoka and the Kalinga war)

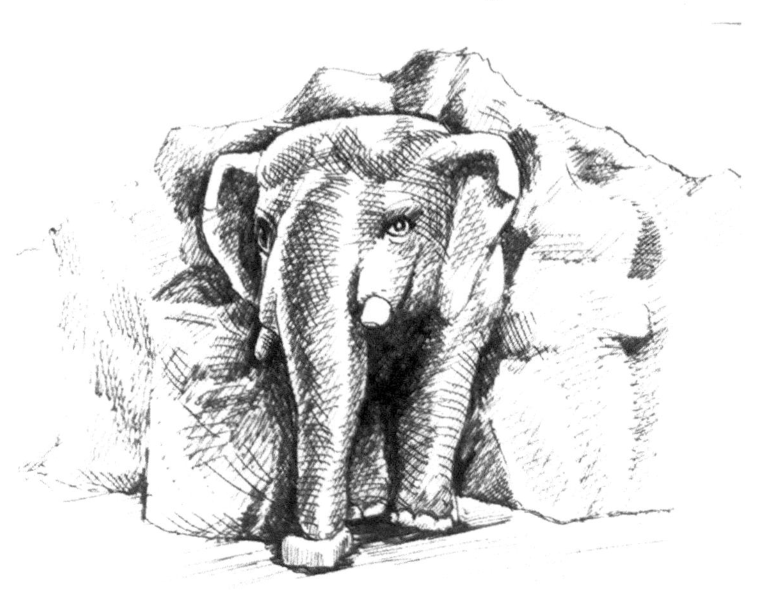

Whisper of the Rock Elephant

(Ashoka and the Kalinga war)

Indramani Jena

Black Eagle Books
USA address:
7464 Wisdom Lane
Dublin, OH 43016

India address:
E/312, Trident Galaxy, Kalinga Nagar,
Bhubaneswar-751003, Odisha, India

E-mail: info@blackeaglebooks.org
Website: www.blackeaglebooks.org

First International Edition Published by
Black Eagle Books, 2024

WHISPER OF THE ROCK ELEPHANT
(Ashoka and the Kalinga war)
by **Indramani Jena**

Cover & Interior Design: Ezy's Publication

ISBN- 978-1-64560-606-2 (Paperback)
Library of Congress Control Number: 2024949698

Printed in the United States of America

Dedication

This treatise is a heartfelt tribute to the countless antiquarians who, with their profound dedication and research, have deciphered the authentic archaeological characters like Piyadasi Ashoka and Mahameghavahana Kharavela. Their efforts have brought to light the true essence of these historical figures from the illegible, worn out ancient scripts, shining a beacon on the pitch dark pages of history.

Author

Kandahar Rock Edict in Aramaic scripts by Piyadasi Raja (Ashoka's) Mandate, 260 B.C. month's after the Deadly Kalinga War

In the eighth of the reign of Piodasses, he conquered Kalinga. A hundred and fifty thousand persons were captured and deported, and a hundred thousand others were killed, and almost as many died otherwise. Therefore, piety and compassion seized him and he suffered grievously. In the same manner wherewith he ordered abstention from living thing, he has displayed zeal and effort to promote piety. And at the same time the king has viewed this with displeasure: of Brahmins and Sramins and others practicing piety who live there [in Kalinga] – and these must be mindful of the interests of the king and must revere and respect their teacher, their father and their mother, and love and faithfully cherish their friends and companions and must use their slaves and dependents as gently as possible – if, of those thus engaged there, any has died or been deported and the rest have regarded this lightly, the king has taken it with exceeding bad grace. And that amongst other people there are ……….."

Translation by REM Wheeler

Foreword

In the annals of human history, a chapter exists so profound, so deeply etched in the collective consciousness of humanity, that it transcends the boundaries of time, race, and creed. It is a tale of power, conquest, triumph, and tragedy woven into the very fabric of existence. At its heart lies the story of Ashoka and the fateful Kalinga War. This momentous event was marked by the triumph of Ashoka's empire over Kalinga. Still, it was also a tragedy, with the war resulting in the deaths of a massive mass of soldiers and civilians. This event reverberates through the corridors of timeand leaves an indelible mark in the hearts of all who witness its unfolding. Now, in the hands of a brave storyteller, this epic saga is brought to life again, its characters and conflicts rendered in vivid detail against the backdrop of ancient India. Prepare to embark on a journey through history, where the lines between heroism and villainy blur and where the actual cost of conquest is bare for all to see. This is a tale of Emperor Ashoka, his queen Karuvaki and the Kalinga War – a story that will captivate and inspire future generations.

As understood through historical research and his rock and pillar edict statements, Ashoka's image is deeply intertwined with the Kalinga War. This pivotal event was the catalyst that transformed him from the pre-Kalinga

War Ashoka to the post-Kalinga War Buddhist preacher we know today.

Antiquarians deciphered Ashoka's rock edicts, which played a crucial role in understanding the significance of the Kalinga War and Ashoka's transformation after that. Piyadasi, the name by which Ashok referred to himself in these inscriptions, was recognized as the king who renounced warfare following his savage massacre in the Kalinga War.

For these antiquarians, discovering the extent and boundaries of ancient Kalinga within the context of British India was of immense importance. At that time, Kalinga's historical memory had primarily faded into obscurity. By meticulously studying Ashoka's inscriptions and comparing them with other historical records, these scholars could piece together the geography and significance of Kalinga in ancient times.

Their efforts shed light on the magnitude of the Kalinga War and its profound impact on Ashoka's worldview. By identifying the region of Kalinga within the broader Indian context, they provided valuable insights into the historical and cultural dynamics of the area during Ashoka's reign.

In essence, the work of these antiquarians helped revive interest in the history of Kalinga and its pivotal role in shaping Ashoka's reign and legacy. It underscores the importance of understanding ancient civilizations and their historical narratives to comprehend the complexities of the past.

Without the Kalinga War, Ashoka's legacy might have been significantly different. He might have been regarded as a competent ruler, somewhere between his grandfather Chandragupta Maurya and his father *Amitraghata* Bindusara in terms of historical significance. However, the profound impact of the Kalinga War on Ashoka's conscience set him apart and elevated him to the status of "Ashoka the Great."

The Kalinga War left Ashoka with intense guilt, remorse, and regret. For two years, he was engulfed in gloom, haunted by the enormity of his actions. His subsequent pilgrimage and encounters with Buddhist teachings further fueled his desire for redemption. With the dedicated devotion and lovingness of his beloved queen, Karuvaki, he could overcome this depression. She worked as a bridge to connect his distressed soul to Buddhism, which, without her effort, would have been unthinkable.

Ultimately, he embraced Buddhism and dedicated himself to spreading its principles of righteousness and compassion. Ashoka's efforts to atone for his past actions were extraordinary. He expanded immense resources and employed his intellect to create a better world, one where his legacy could be defined by his commitment to peace and moral conduct. Despite the bloodshed of the Kalinga War, Ashoka's enduring quest for spiritual growth and enlightenment ultimately defined his legacy as a pious and enlightened ruler.

In the corridors of time, there exists a chapter so poignant, so deeply ingrained in the collective consciousness of humanity, that it defies mere words to capture its essence. This chapter is the tale of Ashoka and the fateful Kalinga War – a momentous event that continues to resonate throughout history. For over two and half years, the land of Kalinga lay shrouded in the shadows of devastation and despair, its people grappling with the aftermath of a conquest that shook them to their core. Yet, amidst the rubble and ruin, there is a conspicuous absence – a void where the name of a king or leader should have stood, adding to the enigma of the historic conflict. And yet, the evidence of Ashoka's presence in Kalinga is undeniable, etched into the landscape at Dhauli and Samapa (Jaugada) in present-day Odisha. The archaeological remnants, scarred by the weight of Ashoka's remorse, serve as a silent testament to the profound impact of his grief, sparking contemplation and introspection in the hearts of all who gaze upon them. For how could a conqueror weep over his victory? And what did he offer in compensation for his grief? These questions linger in the minds of scholars and historians weave a tapestry of intrigue and inquiry that spans the ages. And yet, amidst the complexities of war and repentance, there is a glimmer of redemption – a beacon of hope that shines forth from the depths of Ashoka's soul. In his embrace of Buddhism, he found solace and purpose, dedicating his life to pursuing righteousness and holiness within his kingdom and beyond its borders.

The story of Ashoka and Kalinga stands as a testament to the enduring power of humanity's capacity for introspection and transformation, a reminder that even in the darkness of times, the potential for retrieval and renewal exists. And so, as we delve into the depths of this historic saga, let us not only bear witness to its complexities and contradictions but also seek to uncover the profound truths that lie at its heart.

In this historical novel, the author, known for his expertise in historical fiction, pokes about the enigmatic darkness of a bygone era to explore the reasons behind a victorious Emperor's despair following a hard-won battle. Building upon his acclaimed work Salabhanjika on Kharavela, the author offers a unique perspective on Emperor Ashoka.

This easy-to-read story unfolds through the words of Ashoka himself, reflecting on the proclamations he meticulously crafted over decades. Scrupulously researched and grounded in archaeological evidence, the novel presents a realistic portrayal of the past. Characters, chronology and historical facts are ultra-carefully recreated, drawing upon Kalinga's rich curtains of legends and folktales, all woven into the social fabric of time.

The story promises to satisfy the historian's quest for knowledge and the reader's curiosity and, ultimately, to shed light on the true extent of Ashok's remorse, a historical enigma. But the author's masterful storytelling truly brings this captivating tale to life, ensuring the reader's complete immersion in the narrative.

Prof. Nihar Ranjan Patnaik
Former Director, Higher Education, Odisha and,
Former Professor and Head, Department of History,
Ravenshaw University, Cuttack.
Res: N/2-101, IRC Village, Nayapalli,
Bhubaneswar-751015

Prologue

It's an exceptional event for a victor to experience remorse after emerging triumphant from a monstrous war. Even more extraordinary is the metamorphosis of a once cruel Emperor into a benevolent ruler. Yet, this is the remarkable tale of Ashoka the Great, whose legacy spans over two and half millennia, resurrected from the depths of archaeology.

Once forgotten, Ashoka now commands global recognition, not for the conquests, but for his extensive array of artifacts and rock inscriptions. These relics testify to his benevolent rule, etching his name into the annals of history alongside the great monarchs of old. This global recognition is a source of pride for all who appreciate the depth of history.

Ashoka's legacy, embodied in his rock edicts and proclamations, eclipses the mere exploits of his contemporaries. Yet, as time marched on and the Brahmi script faded into obscurity in the centuries following his reign, Ashoka's name endured. It persisted, awaiting rediscovery by travellers like Fa-Hsien and Hiuen Tsang, unaware of the profound wisdom encapsulated within the ancient inscriptions they beheld.

Emerging from centuries of obscurity, the rediscovery of Ashoka through archaeological endeavours in India unveils a figure vastly different from the descriptions found in Puranic legends and literature. Even authoritative sources remain silent on the brutal Kalinga War, contradicting the stark confessions of the Emperor himself on rock edicts. Amidst a wealth of rock inscriptions and pillar edicts, the historical landscape is veiled in a fog of fictitious narratives and incredulous claims, adding to the enigma of Ashoka's true character.

Among these inscriptions, the Thirteenth Rock Edict is a pivotal Proclamation etched into the western borders of Ashoka's empire in a foreign tongue. Here, the Emperor openly acknowledges the devastation wrought under his command during the Kalinga campaign, a deliberate act either to conceal the edict from notice of Kalinga or to boast to the Western world. Yet, within this confession lies a glimpse into Ashoka's complex personality, humanity, and inner turmoil as he grapples with the concept of sin (*Adhamma*) and the pursuit of righteousness (*Dhamma*). Across the expanse of the empire, these edicts adorn boulders and pillars, imparting sermons on personal conduct, Buddhist principles, administrative strategies, and the intertwining of religion and governance.

The identification of Kalinga and the localization of the war near the base of Dhauli Hill, close to Bhubaneswar in Odisha, provoked a profound sense of pride and reflection among the Odia populace. Rather than focusing solely on the misdeeds of the confessing Emperor, the revelation invokes admiration for the courage displayed by their forebears almost one hundred generations ago. Yet, specific enigmatic phrases within the Proclamation, such as 'Avijit Kalinga', '*Dharma Vaye*', and 'Atavi Lands' continue to perplex Odia readers, inviting them to unravel the cryptic connotations embedded within the epigraphic characters. Each word, laden with historical significance, sparks a journey of contemplation and interpretation, inviting the curious mind to delve deeper into the annals of antiquity.

Immersed in the vast expanse of historical facts and numerous publications, the author embarks on a chronological journey of mental transformation sparked by the archaeological remnants of the Kalinga War. While history often emphasizes the grandeur of monarchs, the war itself is relegated to mere footnotes in Ashoka's inscriptions, encapsulating the essence of its brutality in just a couple of lines. Yet, within the author's mind, this abbreviated account detonates a cascade of reflections, prompting the assembly of fables, folktales and literary accounts from ancient Kalinga and modern Odisha, weaving together a tapestry of history, geography and society.

At the heart of this reconstruction is the figure of the Kalinga woman, or her representative deity, emerging in the aftermath of the war. The author perceives her as a pivotal force capable of catalyzing the transformation of barbarity into righteousness and humanitarianism. Whether she embodies the collective resilience of Kalinga's women, serves as a psychological manifestation within the Emperor's conscience, or represents a divine influence on the human psyche, her presence resonates deeply. This miniature example echoes the transformative journey of figures like the dacoit Dasyu Ratnakar, who evolved into the revered sage Valmiki, author of the epic Ramayana. Throughout history, such metamorphoses abound, illustrating the inherent capacity within humanity.

The story weaves around a pace-making event, a folktale reverberating around Bhubaneswar, Odisha, and the ancient Kalinga capital, Toshali. It narrates the ancient tale of how the victorious yet sinful *Chandashoka* was subdued by the powerful graveyard deity, *Smasan Devi*, and her tantric spells. While it may bring a sense of satisfaction to the inhabitants, this take serves as a poignant reminder of the importance of a human approach over unruliness, trespasser, cruelty and inhumanity. *Janguli,* the name of the deity, is a symbol of woman's power, stood in a place where the graveyards were filled with the fallen.

Through this treatise, the author endeavours to transport the reader to an age shrouded in antiquity and obscurity, where human settlements grappled with the developing concepts of borders and identity. It is a journey that transcends mere historical narrative, delving into the realm of introspection and collective memory, inviting readers to contemplate the fluidity of human nature and the enduring quest for enlightenment amidst the tumult of civilization's infancy.

Contents

It is a historical novel out of the archives of the rock edicts of Emperor Piyadasi – Ashoka Vardhan Maurya. As he is an outcome of archaeology, most of the temporal and spiritual sequences are as per his statements and quotes. Characters are very few as limited to inscriptional publications; spiritual texts are synthesized to fictional character. Few minor characters are there beyond the edicts to complete the contour of the story.

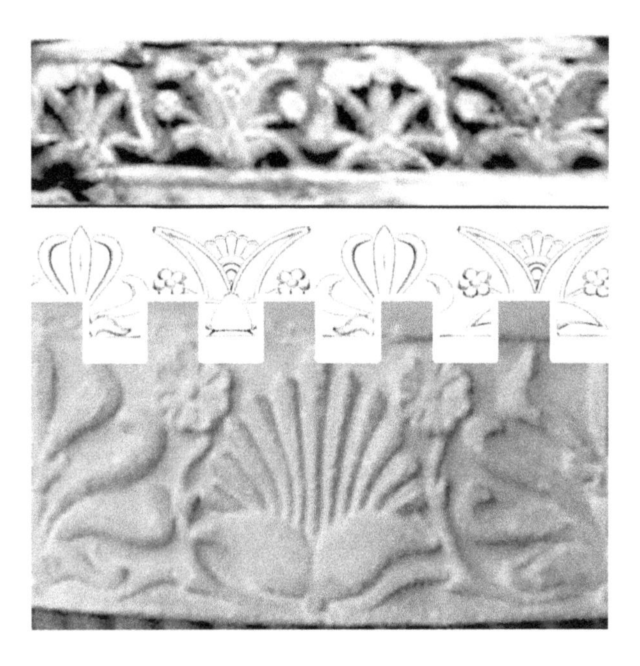

[Mauryan Sculpture]

The Mysterious Encounter with Setu, the Rock Elephant

The two locals, Kalia and Budu, were intrigued when they stumbled upon the rock elephant. They heard a deep, resonating sound reminiscent of a bull's call, yet no bull was in sight. They searched high and low, but the source of the sound remained a mystery. Kalia, a history enthusiast, and Budu, a hospital employee, were both baffled and intrigued, wondering if they were experiencing a shared illusion.

The tall boy among the two was Kalandi, who had the nickname Kalia. The other was Budhiman, whose pet name was Budu, the opposite of his original name. He was knowledgeable and nicknamed a fool due to the innocent appearance of his face.

Kalu had some education up to the intermediate level, but Budu struggled to complete his paramedical practicum and served in a private hospital. Both belonged to the nearby village of Arjuneswara, where the temple of Lord Siva, also known as Arjuneswara, was situated.

But the sound was heard again. It was strange for them. They noted it originated from the rock side where the rock elephant stood with its trunk and two forelegs. The hind part of the elephant was still submerged in the stone mass of the Dhauli Hill. Now, they could be sure what the source was: the whispering of the rock elephant.

[Seto, the Rock Elephant]

The elephant was no recent creation. The two onlookers needed to uncover when it was unearthed from the single rock boulder. Their parents had never seen the carving. But they knew it was as ancient as the three trinity gods of the Vedas - Brahma, Vishnu, and Maheswar, and as mysterious as the whispers of the wind.

They did not take it easy. They have been visitors to the site almost daily for the last few years and are only wondering today. A stone elephant speaking something may be ghost-stricken. They have to avoid this route; otherwise, the spirit of the rock elephant may infest them. They thought the sound they heard would be inauspicious and may invite danger to their mind and body. They decided to avoid this path leading to the mountaintop.

"Listen, my boys, listen! It would help you if you had not panicked. I am revealing something not known to anybody. It will add to your tourist knowledge of the locality of days past. I hope you have the choice to listen to me," a grunt came flowing in the air from the trunk of the rock elephant.

They looked at each other silently, afraid of the curious elephant who might listen to their discussion. They pondered a bit, but Kalu, the tourist guy, had an affirmative expression. He thought the elephant might add something to his guiding menu that would help satisfy the crowd of astutely attentive visitors. Some visitors would be more satisfied with the facts than they see in the tourist spot. He faces several puzzles every day. He may get some patents to answer questions from his clients. But the paramedical guy, Budu, was curious to know something from this unexpected creature that may reveal a marvellous remedy used in days of hoary past!

After a few moments of silence, both talked, putting hands on their mouths lest it may be audible to the elephant: 'We will listen to what the elephant's spirit will tell us but in the daytime. We know this site was a fierce battlefield a thousand years ago, and the people of the village do not dare to pass by this route at night. We feel conscious while trading this route.'

The elephant with big ears had extraordinary hearing capacity and overheard them. He assured, "You need not bother. I will tell a dozen stories about this place, which nobody knows. But you must note that I have seen and heard these events since immemorial. As a rock, I have immense mute witnessing capacity as such. A mighty barbarous king had fought a war with his tent exactly inches ahead of my trunk. He had attempted to construct me in this shape as an inert stony elephant in the land of elephants. The rock seriously objected to his construction, and the sculptors hailing from western foreign land broke all their chisels here on me, and the construction of my shape was halfway as you see today. I see millennia after millennia passing down, but none could give me a full shape. Since then, I have been struggling to escape from the stone mass of the rock. But I have failed to do so; only I had gained my voice, my trumpet, my roaring and my rumbling, my squeaking."

Every day at noon, you come and keep one banana for me. I will tell you something new your textbooks may not tell you, something your research scholars may not dream of. Are you ready with my proposal?"

Both the guys laughed dryly. They agreed but were still frightened, as the same inert part of the elephant had developed a spirit in its soma and wanted to convey something. Their villagers will object to their choice of listening from the rock elephant. It maybe a supernatural object and may misguide the living being. But their decision to keep the conversation a secret allowed them to nod to the proposal.

They answered positively, "Thank you, our precious soul. We will come to worship on Wednesdays with banana and ladu; it is the day of Lord Ganesh. We pray you are aware of something from the hoary past."

The elephant rumbled, "Welcome, my dear patrons. Come to know your hundred-generation ancestors. I will let you know what I have seen and heard. For your impression, I must tell you I happen to be the progeny of *Gajasura,* whose head is transplanted with Lord Ganesh. Your choice of Wednesday is welcome. It is the day of Lord Ganesh you worship."

As the days passed, the allure of the rock elephant's enigma grew more potent. Kalia, the inquisitive guide, saw a chance to expand his knowledge and enthral his tourist clients with new tales of ancient wisdom. Meanwhile, Budu, the paramedic, nurtured aspirations of unearthing hidden remedies and ancient insights that could aid his patients.

On Wednesdays, they returned to the rock elephant, bearing offerings of bananas and ladu, marking the start of a singular bond between man and spirit. They embarked on their weekly pilgrimage with a blend of apprehension and anticipation, eager to delve deeper into the mysteries of the past.

As they approached the rocky outcrop where the rock elephant stood, they felt a sense of reverence and anticipation. The creature greeted them with a rumbling voice, its ancient wisdom resonating.

With each visit, the half-carved-out rock elephant revealed long-forgotten fragments painting vivid portraits of bygone eras and forgotten civilizations. Its tales transported Kalia and Budu to local events of long back, filling their minds with wonder and awe.

But amidst the marvels of the past lurked darker truths and hidden dangers. The rock elephant's warnings of ancient conflicts and vengeful spirits served as a sobre reminder of the perils that lay beyond human understanding.

The rock elephant didn't object to its two patient listeners about his identity. They accepted him as Lord Ganesh of their thought. They conceived him as a representative of the Lord of wisdom; religiously, people of their race trace Lord Ganesh.

But he is different. His mentor did not create him as an ordinary elephant or representative of the Lord of Wisdom. He was built as a white elephant. The albino one is promising, and its name is the *Airabata,* the elephant of Lord *Indradevata* of heaven.

The rock elephant decided to reveal his identity to them at the outset. He did not mind accepting the offerings they had wished for him on Wednesdays.

He started, "Today, you may see me as a part of Lord Ganesh, with my head transplanted onto an elephant's body, revered as a repository of wisdom. But allow me to share an intriguing story that unfolds in a time when *Sanatana Dharma* reigns supreme and Buddhism has waned into obscurity.

My tale begins with a simple inscription, etched at the bottom of the Sixth Rock Edict, in ancient *Brahmi* script and *Pali Prakriti* language, bearing my name: Seto, or as you might interpret it in modern terms, 'Sweta," meaning white, or albino, elephant.

Accept this truth readily, for I am the earliest architectural homage to Lord Buddha in Kalinga. It was created by the skilled sculptors of Magadharaj Piyadasi Ashoka Raja around 250 BC, a decade following his remorse over the ignominious Kalinga War. For two long years, he grappled with his guilt and sorrow, eventually finding solace but remaining haunted by compassion and holiness for the 28 years of his reign.

As a symbol of his atonement, he expressed his remorse in the Thirteenth Rock Edict, deliberately omitting from the vicinity of Kalinga. Instead, he addressed it in a special proclamation dedicated to the region. Here, he professed his love for the people of Kalinga as his children, instructing the royal officials to treat the province with care.

Allow me to elucidate further: Ashoka commissioned my creation at the behest of his second Queen, Queen Consort Karuvaki, who sought to appease the Kalingans by erecting a sacred monument to Lord Buddha on the very site of the Kalinga War. Skilled artisans from the western lands were employed, and I was fashioned from the living rock. Yet, the rock remained a silent witness to the events it had witnessed. Now, endowed with a semblance of consciousness, I can recount the aftermath of the Kalinga War, offering daily insights into its repercussions.

Yet, despite the risks, Kalu and Budu remained steadfast in their quest for knowledge. Guided by the rock elephant's timeless wisdom, they embarked on a journey of discovery that would forever alter their perceptions of the world around them.

In the heart of the wilderness, amid the whispers of ancient spirits and the echoes of forgotten battles, they found a bond that transcended time and space – a bond forged in the crucible of curiosity and illuminated by the light of ancient wisdom. And as they continued their pilgrimage to the rock elephant's rocky domain, they knew their lives would never be the same again.

As Kalu pondered the rock elephant's enigmatic origins, he immersed himself in a divine philosophical contemplation. How could such a celestial phenomenon emerge from the rugged mass of the hill, and why had the carvers left the elephant incomplete? What unseen forces had guided their hands, shaping the creature into its halfway form and halting their progress?

To his astonishment, the half-carved elephant seemed to sense his thoughts, responding with an explanation that transcended the bounds of mortal understanding. According to the creature, the hill itself had opposed the construction of the elephant, its ancient spirit rebelling against the intentions of the once atrocious Emperor, Ashoka. Infused with a sense of holy perspective, the hill had resisted the crooked designs of the Magadharaj, bearing witness to the suffering wrought by his murderous deeds.

Yet, despite the darkness of its past, the rock elephant had been imbued with a higher purpose – a symbol of peace and a testament to the compassionate teachings of Buddha.

Its incomplete form served as a reminder of the spiritual organs of the divine *Airabata,* a beacon of hope amidst the turmoil of the mortal world.

Budu, unable to fully grasp the significance of the elephant's words, watched in awe as Kalu became transfixed by the creature's wisdom. The rock elephant's profound insights penetrated his soul, leaving him pale and shaken.

Sensing their unease, the elephant offered words of reassurance, promising that their journey would lead to enlightenment and understanding. With a sense of reverence, Kalu and Budu bid farewell to the sacred creature, their minds buzzing with anticipation for the revelations that lay ahead.

As they departed, the echoes of the rock elephant's voice lingered in their minds, filling them with a newfound sense of purpose and resolve. In the heart of the wilderness, amidst the whispers of ancient spirits, they had encountered a truth that transcended the boundaries of time and space. The truth would guide them on their journey of discovery and self-discovery.

[Elephant vs. Lion]

The Tall Kalinga Woman in Battlefield

In their second meeting, the rock elephant wanted to depict something that had not taken this form. But he had a presence through the hill boulder, his primitive form. He can see in his divine eyes the proceedings of the era. He intimated that events that happened were so cruel, inhuman and *'adhamma'* that each and everyone would denounce them an unethical war with day and night genocide which was the cause of why the Sun, the Moon and the Sky all cried. Many days, many deaths, men, women, children of Toshali and villages all around, animals, Senapati and tall white infantries of the west on behalf of Magadha – everywhere tones of death.

At the end of the conflict, when the male folk were wiped out, the ladies in a group charged the Magadharaj without fear for life as they had already sacrificed their spouses in huge numbers. This event has been a talk of the press and media since the term Kalinga War was heard from its inscriptional origin; some say it was a Goddess of the cremation ground who tortured the triumphant Magadharaj, Piyadasi Raja, few depict it as a woman exorcist named *'Dhamil'* or *'Janguli'* from the eastern Toshali cremation grounds pounded upon the morally bent down Magadharaj Piyadasi. But I have seen a statuesque approaching the battlefield and daring the Magadharaj left and right, allowing no rescue from moral haunting.

I am, bit by bit, projecting my experience of the unforgettable scene. Be attentive to my picturization –

Amidst the aftermath of the fierce Kalinga War, the once-thriving riverside near Dhauli now bore witness to the ravages of conflict. The air was heavy with the acrid scent of burnt thatch, and the soil was soaked with the blood of countless warriors. The once-peaceful Daya River flowed crimson, starkly reflecting the brutality that had unfolded on its banks.

In surveying the desolation, Emperor Ashoka was overcome by the grim reality of the toll exacted by the war he had waged. His conquest, which had torn through civil areas and spoiled the fertile land, now lay before him as a haunting tableau of destruction. The weight of the consequences settled on his shoulders, and the air echoed with the silent cries of a devastated landscape.

In the sombre setting, a tall Kalinga woman, her eyes swollen with grief, approached the brooding Emperor. She was a poignant silhouette against the backdrop of ruin; her anguish etched in every line of her face. With hands folded and a heart heavy with sorrow, she implored the Emperor to resurrect her fallen family – a husband, a son, and a grandson, all victims of the relentless war.

"Great Emperor," she began, her voice carrying the weight of grief and hope, "I stand before you as a witness to the unforgiving cruelty of this war. My family, my flesh and blood, lie lifeless on this battlefield. They were warriors, like those on both sides, caught in the currents of a conflict, not their making."

Emperor Ashoka, his eyes reflecting the torment within, listened silently as the grieving woman continued her plea. "You, who wield the power of life and death, can you not, in your infinite mercy, restore them to me? Grant them the boon of life, for they fought bravely for their motherland against your might. Today, you, the world's greatest king, hold the key to their destiny. Spare them the eternity of this desolation and let the river of their life flow through their veins once more.

The Emperor, torn between the consequences of his ambition and the depth of his newfound empathy, met her gaze. His silence spoke volumes, a contemplative pause in the aftermath of chaos. With all its brutality, the war had not extinguished the flame of humanity within him. The fate of this grieving woman's family now rested on the precipice of his companion.

The once-ruthless heart that had orchestrated the war now felt pierced by the arrows of remorse. Overwhelmed by the devastation wrought upon the land and its people, Emperor Ashoka felt the burden of guilt settle heavily upon him. With a heavy heart, he lowered his sword to the ground, symbolizing surrender to the weight of his actions.

[The Tall Kalinga Woman]

As the grieving woman pleaded for the resurrection of her fallen family, Emperor Ashoka, in a gesture of deep regret, shook his head in negation. Despite his imperial power, he knew the divine ability to breathe life into the lifeless eluded him. The sorrows of war had transformed the triumphant conqueror into a man grappling with the consequences of his ambition.

The heart-wrenching cry of the grieving woman echoed in the lonely war field. The Emperor, once the embodiment of ruthless power, now stood humbled by the enormity of his actions. The woman, however, no longer cowered in fear. Instead, she raised her voice in defiance and despair, questioning the very essence of the title bestowed upon the remorseful Emperor.

"Can I call you an Emperor or a Murderer?" she cried out, her words a searing indictment of the man who had claimed victory at such a tremendous cost. In response, the bodyguards, loyal to their Emperor, moved forward with swords drawn, ready to silence the defiant woman.

But Emperor Ashoka, acknowledging the weight of her words, intervened. With a solemn command, he ordered his guards to step back and maintain a respectful distance. His eyes, filled with a mixture of sorrow and remorse, met the unwavering gaze of the grieving woman.

Undeterred, she continued her barrage of questions, demanding answers from the once-mighty Emperor, now brought to his knees by the consequences of the war. The war had left scars on the land and chipped away at the veneer of invincibility that once shrouded the powerful ruler.

The tall woman stood amid the war-torn landscape, her anger radiating like an unyielding flame. Strands of dishevelled hair covered her face, and her hands, once tender and caring, were now stained with the fresh blood of her kin. She raised her voice in a fierce lament that echoed across the desolate war field beside the Daya River.

"Magadharaj! What have you wrought upon the sacred soil of Kalinga?" she bellowed her words, a passionate accusation. The pain in her heart translated into a curse, a damning condemnation that reverberated through the air. His fury was not just a personal outcry but a collective expression of the suffering endured by Kalinga's women, a curse that would echo through the ages.

In the wake of the relentless war, she painted a vivid picture of the atrocities committed by the conqueror. The massacre had spared no one, young or old, leaving a trail of destruction that touched every aspect of life. Once fertile and vibrant, the land was rendered uninhabitable, scarred by the brutality you inflicted upon it. The Emperor's actions had disrupted the natural order, poisoning the very essence of existence.

The tall woman, her eyes blazing with anger, continued her curse. "Your merciless murder of a race is the curse for Kalinga women," she declared, her voice carrying the weight of centuries of suffering. She held the conqueror accountable for the destruction of her people, invoking the wrath of gods who, she believed, would never excuse such inhumanity.

With each word, she etched a curse that transcended time, a testament to the enduring pain of a nation violated. Her curse was a plea to the divine forces, a call for justice against a ruler who had plunged her land into darkness. The once-mighty Emperor, now confronted by the consequences of his actions, stood before her as a symbol of remorse, haunted by the curse of a grieving woman whose anguish echoed through the ages.

The tall woman, her once-flowing hair now dishevelled, stood amidst the grim aftermath of the war. Her hands and forehead stained with the blood of her kin, she unleashed a torrent of anger and grief upon the conqueror. The Emperor, now confronted by the consequences of his actions, listened in stunned silence as the woman cursed him.

"Magadharaj!"You have reproduced a giant Ashoka-Hell of your place here in Kalinga." She thundered, a searing indictment of the Emperor's brutal conquest. The curse she uttered was not just a personal lament but a collective cry of anguish from Kalinga's women, a curse that transcended time.

"Your merciless murder of a race is the curse for Kalinga women," she declared, her voice echoing with the weight of the suffering endured by her people. The once-fertile land was now tainted, the food and water poisoned by the atrocities committed in the name of conquest. The Emperor, now seen as the architect of this devastation, stood before her as a symbol of inhumanity.

"What have you created in this golden land on earth?" she continued, her rage unabated. "You have smashed people of all ages, spoiled the food and water, and made the land uninhabitable! God can't excuse you for your inhumanity and blunder."

Still grappling with the enormity of his deeds, the Emperor muttered, "How are women affected in this war?" His question, seemingly oblivious to the suffering he had caused, further fuelled the woman's anger.

"Deliberately, you have created a plot of genocide in Kalinga," she roared, her voice a fierce retort. "You have turned this land into a hell, much like the Ashoka Hell you have built at your Pataliputra capital. It is the fate you carry since your birth. Your blood thirst has made me a widow, son and grandson devoid. Their carcasses at the other end of the battlefield are a heart-rending scene for me." The conversation unfolded in a crescendo of sorrow and accusation as the tall woman laid bare the atrocities inflicted upon her and her people by the Emperor's ruthless campaign of war.

The woman who had an acute sense of hearing, seemed to catch the Emperor's muted musings. "It might be your misfortune. Is an Emperor responsible for the result of a war?"

Suppressing her grief, she unleashed her voice in a thunderous retort, "Damn you, cruel, impious hell! Murder is your habit, just as your family life is discussed among your subjects. You are looked upon as less than an insect from the standpoint of humanity."

The Emperor was then stunned into silence and confronted by the Kalinga woman's piercing accusations. Her words, an unyielding condemnation of his character and actions, cut through the air with a force that left him speechless. The woman's vehement denunciation exposed the Emperor's moral weakness, laying bare the disintegration of his mental integrity.

The once-mighty ruler, now faced with the consequences of his ruthless campaign, felt a weight upon his conscience. His face turned pale, and he stood disoriented, grappling with the reality of the devastation he had wrought upon Kalinga. The Woman's voice, fuelled by grief and anger, echoed across the war-torn field, challenging the core of the Emperor's being.

"**Give back my husband, son, and grandson alive**! You did not engage in a face-to-face war with the formidable elephants of Kalinga, capable of smashing your Magadha forces, your strongholds at Takshashila and Ujjain, and your hired military from the west. What charges do you bring against my relations that made them victims of your genocide? What harm had they done to you?"

The Emperor, overwhelmed with remorse, faced an unprecedented dilemma. He had revelled in the pleasure of torture and murder, finding joy in the suffering and bleeding bodies of his victims. Now, confronted by the tragic lady of Kalinga, he was challenged to consider the unthinkable – bringing the dead back to life, an impossible feat. The realization that he lacked the power to redress the woman's grievances struck him profoundly. He grappled with the awareness that ill-treating and killing a man were grave sins, not easily forgiven.

His complexion turned even paler, beads of sweat formed on his forehead, and his hands trembled, reflecting the turmoil within. His eyes drooped with guilt, and he teetered on the verge of collapse. The guards rushed to his aid, helping him regain composure and stand upright. The Emperor gestured for them to return to their previous positions.

The woman, however, remained unappeased by the Emperor's distress. Her grief refused to subside, and she cared little for her own life as she confronted the assassin responsible for the destruction of her family. Even the prospect of death at the hands of the guards held no fear for her; her only concern was ensuring the Emperor faced the consequences he deserved. She continued her relentless barrage of questions, unmoved by the unfolding drama.

"Magadharaj! Who has instilled in you the habit of torturing fellow beings and delighting in the suffering of life? Are you not the esteemed son of the virtuous Magadha Rajamata and the father, Bindusar, known as Amitraghata, a friendly and humane soul? What has led to your inhumane attitude and the pleasure you derive from shedding blood? You utilized all your might to transform Kalinga into an Ashoka Hell!" the woman paused in her curse.

The guards, unable to tolerate any further, raised their weapons, aiming for the woman's forehead. However, before they could proceed, an unseen force held them back. It was as if an invisible hand had restrained them. Once standing proud, the Emperor was now kneeling on the battlefield in front of the woman, his sword partly dipping into the sandy soil. The atmosphere along the lover shore, usually filled with the sounds of war, now held a pin-drop silence. No one could discern who had stopped the guards. The scene was intolerable for the Magadha guards, representing a kingdom known for its aggressiveness and ruthlessness in battle.

The truth had triumphed. The Emperor's position against the backdrop was a miraculous admission of guilt as the assassin of Kalingans. What else could a demoralized soul resort to? However, the fury of the Kalinga woman remained unabated. Even if the Emperor were to beg for pardon from humanity, God, and the earth, she could not see the possibility of such a recitation from the mouth of the sinner. She was sure that if he did not acknowledge his guilt, he would spend his entire life tormented by guilt, haunted by the shadows of his misdeeds, and seeking self-correction and redemption.

However, this admission was not enough to forgive an Emperor responsible for the lives and well-being of his subjects and the administration of justice.

The Emperor of Magadha, overwhelmed by the weight of his guilt, dropped to his knees with closed eyes, unable to face the barrage of questions from the tall and mourning woman. Fuelled by revenge, she sought to inflict deep and lasting wounds on his psyche, ensuring that mental scars would endure as long as his devilish body survived. Her earnest desire was to make him comprehend the boundaries of humanity and humanitarian practices, preventing him from ever raising his sword again.

The two royal attendants, mesmerized by the unfolding scene, deliberated on the Emperor's action. One of them, perhaps influenced by loyalty, suggested that their Emperor should not confess to anything. They hastily carried him to a nearby military tent a few yards away. Though he had not wholly lost consciousness, he was deeply enthralled, temporarily losing his sense of self and groping for it in the intangible air. The once most important ruler on earth was demoralized by realizing his inhuman deeds.

Meanwhile, the tall woman gazed at the ground, lamenting the irreparable loss in her life. Her blame extended beyond the scolding, and she directed at the Emperor, focusing more on her face. She was in a surreal situation, confronting an Emperor, a scenario far removed from the usual grandeur of royal palaces and battlefields.

Regarding some semblance of consciousness and courage, the Emperor decided to face the woman. In a mechanical tone, he ordered his attendants, "Take back to my place in front of that lamenting woman. At the very least, I must endure some of her scolding to solace her wounded feelings."

The Emperor, no longer concerned with the specific address of the woman, was convinced that she represented the collective voice of the women of Kalinga. Whatever grievances she articulated were likely shared by all the women in a country transformed into a vast battlefield.

He regretted not heeding the repeated warnings from his second queen Karuvaki, who had advised him against attacking innocent Kalinga, cautioning him about a political misunderstanding.

His regret was profound. In addition to shattering Kalinga's human and natural resources, he had tarnished his reputation as a man. He now lacked prestige in the eyes of civilized societies, royal races, Mauryan foreign delegates, and all well-wishers. While nature would eventually restore Kalinga over a century, and its peoples would rebuild from the remnants, the Emperor questioned whether the present and future civilizations of humanity would ever forgive him for the crimes he had committed.

In a moment of introspection, he loudly instructed, "Hey Mahat, hey Sevak, carry me back to my place near the small plant where the woman is mourning. Let me listen to her grief and endure her verbal assaults for the heinous crime I have committed."

Both attendants found themselves in a perplexing situation. They were hesitant to carry out the Emperor's orders, but the weight of his words left them with no choice. Lifting him onto a stretcher, they transported him to the dwarf Ashoka plant, where the grieving woman stood in silence. Though he had regained some courage, the Emperor couldn't bring himself to face the bold woman directly.

As the woman ceased crying, she calmly conveyed that Kalinga had not been completely shattered. It endured in the Atavika forests, armed with staunch archery. Unlike the Emperor's cowardly approach, the people of Kalinga engaged in principled warfare, giving notice and confronting their adversaries face to face. She accused the Emperor of waging a ruthless war without discrimination, indiscriminately claiming lives in every village, paddy field and forest.

Perceiving a shift from lamentation to retaliation in the woman's tone, the Emperor recognized a form of psychological recovery. Summoning his courage, he dared to meet her gaze. However, instead of finding solace, he was met with a torrential flow of abuses.

The woman was astonished to witness the Emperor standing tall, seemingly unaffected by her scathing words. Unperturbed, she continued her verbal assault, commanding him to disappear from her sight. The statuesque branded him a Magadha demon incapable of being a benevolent king. She accused him of being a blood-sucking satan, questioning his ability to measure up to the poorest man on earth in terms of humanity. In her eyes, he was nothing more than a scandalized Emperor.

Emperor absorbed her tirade in silence, choosing not to respond to her provocations. He understood she was using words like pungent lime to paint his wounds. Throughout her tirade, her voice wavered with intermittent laments. Consoling herself and wiping away tears, she occasionally pulled her long hair away from her face. Memories of her lost relations plunged her into deep mourning. Suddenly, she shifted to furious shouts directed at the Emperor, punctuated by sporadic sarcastic laughter.

"Don't revel in the false pride of acquiring Kalinga. You are still incapable of truly possessing the kingdom. Did you manage to capture the King of Kalinga? Despite your attempts to coerce surrender through your emissaries, what audacity do you have to force a king to submit before the Mauryas? Kalinga proposed an alternative – autonomous status with the King of Kalinga as a friend of Magadha, a *Mitra Rashtra*. Kalinga was not afraid of your father or grandfather; they were men. But this progeny of a demon may wreak havoc on the whole world, yet he cannot subdue the King of Kalinga!"

The woman, addressing him as the sovereign of Magadha, condemned him for wielding the power of the earth to obliterate a once prosperous kingdom without rhyme or reason. She questioned the purpose of life in the wake of such devastation and pleaded with him to end her suffering by cutting her throat with his sword.

The Emperor, startled by the woman's unexpected insights and audacity, realized she was no ordinary inhabitant of Kalinga. Her knowledge and understanding of the political landscape suggested that the situation might be more precarious than initially thought despite Magadha's hard-earned victory. The fear loomed that the people of Takshashila and Ujjain, previously prone to riots, could unite with remnants of the Kalinga King, jeopardizing the newly acquired conquest.

In a moment of daring curiosity, the Emperor impulsively posed a question to the absent woman, addressing her as "Sister," He hesitated to call her sister, fully aware that he was the cause of her husband's murder. Nevertheless, he ventured to inquire, "Sister, can you guess the whereabouts of the Kalinga King?"

As he spoke, he realized the woman had departed from the battlefield, leaving no trace behind. Only her echoing scoldings persisted, reverberating through the air. The dwarf tree nearby, remained silent, unable to offer any insight. The Emperor, haunted by the woman's words, couldn't shake the feeling that she would continue to haunt his conscience, holding him accountable for the destruction he wrought upon Kalinga. Despite the fear, he harboured a desperate desire to extract information from her about the elusive Kalinga King, a figure they had been unable to locate despite the complete upheaval of the kingdom.

Kalu and Budu were utterly captivated by the tale. The realization that humanity and vanity once adorned the society of Kalinga a staggering two millennia ago was beyond their comprehension. They were left stunned at the monstrous nature of Emperor Ashoka, a revelation that came to light after the devastating Kalinga War.

As Seto elaborated, the Kalinga tall woman's story could represent the conscience collective. This figure not only serves as a warning to the human conscience but despises the attitude so intensely that even an Emperor would weep in sorrow for the pronounced term, which may last until he survives, striving to rectify himself.

It is the perpetual ebb and flow of human conscience, a force that remains steadfast even in our contemporary era.

Both of them thanked the divine soul and dispersed.

[Elephant with Archers]

The Guilty Emperor

As Kalu and Budu embarked on their journey to meet the rock elephant again, anticipation buzzed like perceptible energy. They carried offerings of ladu and another for reverence, eager to continue their conversation with the enigmatic creature.

Their path to the hill was familiar yet imbued with excitement and wonder. Along the way, they passed by the Peace Pagoda, a majestic structure erected by the Japan Nippon Society in memory of the Kalinga War and as a sacred ground dedicated to the teachings of Buddha. The presence of such a monument served as a poignant reminder of the region's tumultuous past and its enduring commitment to peace and spirituality.

As they approached the rocky outcrop where the rock elephant stood, their hearts quickened with anticipation. They knew that within its ancient form lay the wisdom of ages waiting to be imparted to those willing to listen.

Kalu, ever the historian at heart, mused on the countless individuals who had passed through this sacred site over the centuries. Stone diggers, sculptors, scribes, and administrators had left their mark on the land, their stories interwoven with the fabric of time. The Maurya rule had brought a wave of Buddhist influence, transforming Kalinga into a hub of spiritual activity and enlightenment.

[Piyadasi]

With each step closer to the rock elephant, Kalu and Budu felt a sense of reverence and awe wash over them. They knew that they were about to embark on a journey of discovery that would unveil their ancestors' hidden truths and shed light on the mysteries of the past.

As they reached the foot of the hill, they paused for a moment to take in the sight before them. The ancient rock elephant stood silent and imposing, its weathered form a witness to the passage of time. And as they prepared to engage in conversation once more, they felt a deep sense of gratitude for the opportunity to commune with the wisdom of the ages.

The rock elephant thanked them for their punctuality and interest in listening to the story of the period of yore. At once, it started the story.

The atmosphere was laden with unease and

apprehension as the victorious Emperor commented on his homebound journey. Despite the strong security measures in place, the lingering fear of potential attacks from remnants of Kalinga resistance weighed heavily on the minds of the Magadha guards and officials.

The *Senapati*'s arrival at the Toshali Camp signalled the urgency of Emperor Ashoka's return to the capital. However, amidst his deep remorse and dismay, the Emperor remained oblivious to the messages and arrangements being made on his behalf. His emotional turmoil was perceptible, his once-regal demeanour replaced by the vulnerability of a troubled soul.

Preparations were swiftly made for the journey back to Pataliputra, the heart of the Maurya Empire. Accompanied by his trusted driver, Sumanta, and a cavalry contingent, the Emperor embarked on the familiar path homeward. The landscape, scarred by the recent war, bore witness to the devastation wrought upon Kalinga.

Yet, amidst the physical journey, Emperor Piyadasi was beset by the relentless torment of his conscience. The haunting image of the tall Kalinga woman, her piercing questions echoing in his mind, agonizing him ceaselessly. He grappled with the weight of his actions, his once resolute countenance now clouded with doubt and remorse.

The Emperor's introspection deepened as the journey progressed along the forested road, away from the coastal route and the bustling port of Tamralipi. The rugged terrain mirrored his turmoil; each bump and turn reminded him of the challenges ahead.

In this state of emotional disarray, Emperor Piyadasi's journey home became not just a physical passage but a metaphorical odyssey of redemption and self-discovery. The road ahead was uncertain, but he knew he must traverse it to confront the consequences of his actions and seek solace for his troubled soul.

As the victorious Emperor journeyed homeward, a faint glimmer of hope struggled to pierce through the overwhelming darkness of his worried mind. Despite Magadha's triumph in battle, the victory felt hollow and empty, tainted by the atrocities committed during the war. The weight of his conscience bore down heavily on him, drowning out any semblance of joy or satisfaction.

The haunting voice of the tall woman from Kalinga echoed incessantly in Ashoka's mind, her accusations of genocide piercing through his thoughts like shards of glass. Her words served as a relentless reminder of the brutal reality of the war and the bloodshed it had unleashed upon the land.

In a desperate attempt to reconcile his actions with his conscience, Ashoka rationalized victory as the inevitable outcome of conquest. He urged himself to embrace the triumph and overlook how it had been achieved. Yet, the woman's voice continued to resound, stripping away any façade of justification and leaving him bare before the harsh truth of his misdeeds.

As the journey progressed, a sudden obstacle halted their path – a blockade erected in the Ashoka's men, a tactical manoeuvre to control the flow of people and prevent interference in the battle. Forced to seek an alternative route, they found themselves in a deserted village, its charred remnants bearing witness to the violence that had consumed it.

The sight of the widowed women, their bangles shattered and forehead devoid of vermillion they beautify as signs of married Kalinga wife, spoke volumes of the dreadful tragedy that had befallen them. Ashoka's heart clenched with guilt as he contemplated the suffering he might have unwittingly caused. His conscience wrestled with the consequences of his actions for which he was solely responsible.

As the women fled into the forest, seeking refuge from the Emperor's perceived threat, Ashoka was left to confront the harsh reality of his legacy. The anguish of their plight gnawed at his soul, leaving him with a sense of profound remorse and uncertainty.

In that moment of introspection, as the cart turned towards back the main road, Ashoka confronted the painful truth of his reign. The road ahead was fraught with external and internal challenges, and he knew that redemption could only be found through the arduous journey of atonement and reconciliation.

The coachman, Sumanta, spurred the horses frantically along the main road from Toshali to Pataliputra, a journey that seemed to stretch on for infinity. They had only to cover merely six hours of the journey, maintaining a steady speed of an average of two yojans (16 miles, 25 km) per *ghadi* or *muhurta* of time. Thankfully, they stumbled upon a well-maintained seasonal road, a godsend that allowed them to navigate the forested terrain with relative ease– dried-up streams providing a clear path in the late spring.

Despite the improved road conditions, the Emperor remained visibly uneasy. The sight of the cleared pathways, evidence of the recent military campaign in Kalinga, failed to provide him solace. He bore the weight of responsibility for the ferocity of the assault upon Kalinga, the guilty conscience he could not shake off. His conscience relentlessly condemned him, refusing to grant him absolution.

After a brief pause, the Emperor urged Sumanta to

resume their journey. They reached a village nestled along a winding forest path as they continued north. They noted a settlement with a pond, temple and cottages. The town was an important business centre. To their dismay, the settlement lay in ruins, engulfed in smoke from recent fires. The devastation was visible under broad daylight, with no signs of life amidst the destruction. The Emperor witnessed the damage to the town not long back, maybe two or three days ago. The smoke had not yet extinguished from the heaps of thatches. Seeing the aftermath of his decision, the Emperor grappled with overwhelming guilt and remorse.

It was the third instance that shook the base of his conscience. This harrowing scene compounded the Emperor's anguish, driving home the consequences of his actions. He acknowledged his guilt in destroying Kalinga, a kingdom he had sought to integrate into the Magadha Empire, not reduce to ashes. He reflected on the brutality of conquest, where the powerful wielded their might without regard for ethics or humanity.

His mind peeped to utter; it happened in every case where a greater power conquers an unconquered kingdom. The powerful exert all their powers and go beyond the ethics of war. The minor power has two options – to surrender as docile or to fight as brave, even to the last living person. Kalinga opted for the latter to defend until the last drop of blood. It is undoubtedly indomitable and courageous, and its bravery would stand as a brilliant example in the pages of history.

He had experiences of ruthlessly suppressing the rebellions of the interior of the Maurya Empire in Avantirath and Takshashila. Still, the atrocity inflicted on an independent kingdom was an event unseen and unheard of in history. However, channelling the three contingents from these two provinces and the capital to unconquerable Kalinga in three different tracts had trisected the geography of human settlements. No man, royal, or foreign land will spare Magadha and Piyadasi from such vandalism.

As they prepared to depart, the black ashes still dropping down its soiled carriage wheels, the cries of orphaned children struck the Emperor, their wails piercing the melancholy air. Compassion overwhelmed him; tears streamed down his cheeks, rendering him speechless. He felt powerless in the face of such profound suffering, unable to offer comfort or solace to the grieving mothers and their innocent children.

In a poignant moment, a tall woman, smudged with soot, instructed the caretakers to shield the orphans from the Emperor's gaze. Her words struck a chord within him, intensifying his inner turmoil. Sumanta, recognizing the Emperor's distress, resolved to ensure the welfare of the injured and needy children, offering what little solace he could amidst the devastation.

As the sun set on the horizon, casting a pail of darkness over the land, the Emperor was seizing hold of the horror of his actions. Alone with his conscience, he confronted the stark reality of his role in the tragedy that had befallen Kalinga. Despite his desire to escape the anguish that consumed him, there was no refuge from the consequences of his decisions.

They commenced their northward journey after spending the night in a military camp near the former Kalinga-Magadha border. The camp was situated on the outskirts of an urban settlement in Kalinga renowned for its Jain temple and religious centre. This town had significance for over two centuries, mainly since Bardhamana Mahavira visited Kalinga and Kumarigiri. It served as a *Digambara*

Jain sanctuary, home to numerous *Yapannapaka* mendicants.

As their carriage departed from the outskirts of the town, they encountered the Jain temple at the northern boundary. The sight that met their eyes was horrifying: the temple grounds were strewn with lifeless bodies of murdered *Yapannapaka* monks. These monks belonged to a rigorous sect known for their strict dietary practices and minimal attire. The temple itself lay in ruins, its flag reduced to ashes.

Though not devout, Emperor Piyadasi was deeply affected by the scene before him. While he recognized his familial connection to Jainism through his grandfather and father, he understood that waging war against the independent kingdom did not necessitate an assault on its religious institutions. War is a fire for religions; they are vulnerable to melting at the beginning of war.

Unable to pass by, the carriage came to a halt amidst the stench of death emanating from the monk's corpses. The Emperor was moved with intense feelings of remorse, acknowledging his role in the tragic loss of life. The revered monks, who had dedicated their lives to serving society, had fallen victim to the swords of the Magadha army. He judged his position in the measure of '*Dhamma-Adhamma*' balance, and this religious atrocity filled him with melancholy.

The gravity of the situation left Sumanta, the coachman, at a loss for words. Despite being a devout Buddhist, he found himself troubled by the brutality of the military campaign. He likened the Emperor's experience to that of Gautama Buddha, who had been profoundly impacted by witnessing the bare realities of human suffering from an older man, a sick man, a corpse and a wandering renunciant. Providence had arranged a harsher show for the Emperor wrought by him.

For Piyadasi, the encounter with the decapitated monks marked the fourth episode of the artificial disaster he had to witness. It followed encounter with a grieving woman, a village of widows and a settlement of helpless orphans. These experiences weighed heavily on his conscience, plunging him into a profound state of despair.

As they entered Magadha's interior, Sumanta decided no more pathetic story would come. Even though traces did appear, he was determined to proceed without any break on the plea of vehicular limitations. He would reach the palace early.

The rock elephant completed the day's tale and looked at the guys.

They were deeply affected by the tale of inhuman action that had spread to the interior villages of Kalinga, and they could imagine the immense loss inflicted by the Black Piyadasi of Magadha. The battle-scarred settlements shattered the heart of the Kalinga; life, property and the environment were all brutally ravaged. Once a glow of light, the unconquered kingdom now bore witness to the worst havoc wrought by fellowmen. Yet, in the face of this devastation, they felt a fire ignite within them, a fire that made them willing to lay down their lives for the sake of the motherland. Kalinga's patriotism, a flame that burned brighter than any other, proved to be unparalleled in history.

With sorrowful faces, tearful eyes and grimaces on their foreheads, they bid farewell to the rock elephant.

Kalinga Victory Celebration

As Budu and Kalu made their way to the Dhauli Hill to meet the rock elephant again, their excitement bubbled over, fueled by their addiction to the tales spun by the ancient rock creature. Despite arriving much earlier than their scheduled meeting time, they were eager to begin their conversation, having already prepared offerings to show their reverence.

During their journey, Budu couldn't contain his wonder at the supernatural nature of the rock elephant. His curiosity was piqued, and he questioned Kalu about the source of the creature's extraordinary powers. Kalu, ever the knowledgeable guide, explained that the rock elephant, known as Seto, possessed divine attributes beyond those of a mere earthly elephant. Seto was believed to be the albino elephant of heaven, the *Airabata,* the celestial conveyance of Lord Indra. With its omniscient abilities, Seto could perceive past events and even foresee the future, offering glimpses into the hidden truths of history.

Arriving at their destination, Budu and Kalu greeted the rock elephant with deep reverence, following the local custom of bowing with foreheads touching the ground. Placing their offerings of ladu on the rock elephant's trunk, they felt awe as they sensed the ancient creature's response, seemingly stirred by their gesture.

The rock elephant acknowledged their sincerity and

curiosity and expressed appreciation for their dedication to unravelling the past mysteries. With a rumbling voice that echoed with ancient wisdom, it recounted the next chapter in its tale, its emotions perceptible as it delved into the events of bygone eras.

Budu and Kalu listened intently as the story unfolded, their minds transported to a time long before their own, where the mountains stood as silent witnesses to the ebb and flow of history. With each word the rock elephant spoke, they felt a deep connection to the past, their souls stirred by the timeless truths revealed in its ancient tales. And as they sat at the feet of the rock elephant, enveloped in its presence, they knew that their thirst for knowledge would never be quenched, for the mysteries of the past were infinite, waiting to be discovered by those willing to listen.

As Emperor Piyadasi reached Pataliputra, the grand capital of Magadha, a magnificent arrangement awaited him. The city was adorned with banners and decorations, celebrating the return of the victorious Emperor who had subdued the arch-rival in a glorious conquest. The streets were lined with cheering crowds, eagerly awaiting the sight of their triumphant Maharaja.

The Chief Minister, Mukhya Amat Radhagupta, and a host of royal officials and subjects had assembled to greet the Emperor. A splendid gate adorned with colourful flowers and a lion symbol had been erected to mark his arrival in the capital city.

"Congratulations, our Emperor! Congratulations!" echoed the jubilant voices of the crowd as the Emperor's royal entourage approached the gate. Slogans and cheers filled the air as the procession approached the palace, where a grand reception awaited.

But amidst the festivities, the Emperor appeared pale and sad. His countenance was marked by a profound sadness, noticeable to all. While the assembled subjects attributed his demeanour to the rigors of the long journey and travel fatigue, they remained unaware of the deep turmoil within the Emperor's soul.

Calling aside Radhagupta, the Emperor whispered hoarsely, "I am not feeling well. Take me to the palace by the shortest route."

Thus, the procession hastened to the palace, where the Chief Queen and the royal attendants awaited to offer their congratulations. The Chief Queen, hoping to lift Emperor's spirits, presented him with bouquets of fragrant jasmine flowers, a gesture meant to welcome him after months of arduous warfare.

However, the Emperor's response was unexpected. "Leave me alone in my chamber," he murmured, his voice heavy with desolation. "Close the doors and windows. I need solitude."

Ganga, the venerable caretaker of the palace and a witness to Piyadasi's upbringing, observed the profound change in the Emperor's demeanour with growing concern. Never before had he seen him in such a state of despair. The young prince, known for his strength and decisiveness, now appeared broken and inconsolable.

As Ganga silently attended to his duties, he couldn't help but ponder the cause of Piyadasi's grief. The grief was not the reaction he had expected from a victorious ruler returning from battle. The palace, which would typically be alive with jubilation and revelry, now felt heavy with sorrow and uncertainty.

Ganga's mind raced with questions, his heart heavy with concern for the pathos-stricken Emperor. What unseen burdens weighed upon Piyadasi's soul, driving him to such depths of despair? It was a mystery that left Ganga bewildered and troubled, unsure how to offer solace to his troubled monarch. He had seen all Maurya Emperors, from Grandfather to this grandson. Whenever they won a war, by might or diplomacy, they were cheered, and the palace was all cheerful and dancing for at least one year of celebration. He had a great puzzle in his mind to understand this wicked boy before him who did not hesitate to kill animals and living creatures and get pleasure out of it.

The Emperor found little relief from the ache in his body as his mind weighed heavily with an oppressive darkness, like an overcast sky before a storm. Despite his longing for rest, the tumult within his mind raged on, preventing him from finding solace even in sleep. Heavy with weariness, his eyelids refused to close fully, betraying the turmoil. With spells of transient unconsciousness, his mind transported him back to the scene of the orphaned children he had encountered on his journey home. He saw once again the pool of blood, a grim reminder of the atrocities of war, and heard the haunting cries of the children as they recoiled from the tainted waters. There, amidst the blood-stained landscape, stood the tall woman of Dhauli her form transformed into that of a divine deity adorned with a garland of human skulls.

Her gaze bore into him, filled with a wrath that seemed to emanate from the depths of the underworld. The Emperor awoke with a start, his heart pounding with fear and guilt. He felt as though a legion of vengeful spirits surrounded him, each accusing him of the crimes committed in the name of conquest.

In his delirium, he cried out defiantly, denying any wrongdoing and asserting his authority as the ruler of

Magadha. But deep down, he knew the truth – he bore the burden of responsibility for the horrors unleashed upon Kalinga.

As the late afternoon sun cast its dwindling rays over the palace, the Emperor's anguished cries echoed through the halls, reaching the ears of those nearby. Ganga, even vigilant, relayed the Emperor's distress to the Chief Queen, who stood nearby, her heart heavy with concern for her troubled husband.

The Emperor was engulfed in a terrible ache that seemed to permeate his body and mind, casting a heavy shadow over his being as an overcast sky. Despite his longing for rest, the tumultuous storm raging within his mind's eye refused to grant him respite. His eyelids fluttered open and shut, resembling those of a startled bull, yet his gaze remained inward, detached from the world around him. Any glimmer of cheer that had once resided in the recesses of his mind was now obscured by a veil of grim despair.

Unintentionally, his eyes closed for a fleeting moment, perhaps just a few blinks, and he found himself nestled within the haunting imagery of the orphaned children he had encountered on his journey back from Kalinga. In his mind's eye, he witnessed a blood-soaked pond surrounded by the emaciated bodies of innocent victims, their terror evident as they recoiled from crimson waters tainted by the blood of their loved ones. The voices of the tall woman from Kalinga, who had bombarded him with relentless questions on the battlefield, kept pounding in his ears.

She materialized before him, not as a warrior but as a haunting figure, her garlands of human skulls a chilling site. Her presence carried an otherworldly weight, her gaze penetrating the Emperor's soul, stirring a primal fear that forced him to avert his eyes, seeking refuge from her spectral inquisition.

"Have you performed a righteous deed?" Her ethereal voice reverberated within the confines of his mind, piercing through the layers of his consciousness with an unrelenting force.

"No, no, it is not Kalinga, it is Magadha. I am the Emperor. You have no authority here," the Emperor muttered weakly, his words a feeler's attempt to banish the spectre of guilt that haunted him.

But her words lingered, echoing in the depth of his being, stirring dormant fears and igniting a sense of dread that threatened to consume him. The spectre of his past actions loomed large, casting a dark shadow over his conscience as he grappled with the weight of his transgressions.

"Perhaps you are here in Magadha, but what of the afterworlds? Will you escape the sins you have wrought upon humanity? Every drop of blood spilt cries out for justice, demanding retribution in this life and the next," her voice echoed within him, a relentless reminder of the consequences of his actions.

Struggling to rise, the Emperor was overcome by a wave of dizziness that sent him reeling and forced him to retreat into his bed. The horrors of his past deeds continued to haunt him, the spectral presence looming giant as he wrestled with the demons of his own making.

He turned his side, but in vain, his reeling accentuated, and he had to roll back to the wall side.

The Emperor's non-response and withdrawal symptoms deeply concerned Ganga, the principal caretaker of his room. Despite the Emperor's warning, Ganga felt helpless despite his master's listlessness, groaning, and delirium. Realizing the seriousness of the situation, he sought assistance from the Chief Queen, who resided just a few yards away in the women's block of the palace. With a sense of urgency, he hurried towards her quarters, the wooden platform of the palace echoing with his hasty steps.

Before he could knock on the door, the Queen opened it swiftly, alerted by the commotion. Ganga relayed the situation's urgency to her without wasting a moment.

"Your Highness! Kindly rush to the Emperor's room. He is unwell and unresponsive to me. I can't discern the nature of his illness. He is restless and delirious, muttering incomprehensible words," he explained urgently.

The Queen wasted no time and immediately accompanied Ganga to the Emperor's room. With a gentle and concerned tone, she addressed the Emperor.

"Your Majesty, shall I summon our Chief Royal Physician, the *Raja Vaidya*, to attend to your ailment?" She inquired softly.

To her surprise, the Emperor responded with groans, questioning the assumption of his illness.

The Queen, undeterred, explained her concern for his well-being, emphasizing his withdrawal and incoherent muttering as signs of distress.

However, the Emperor dismissed the notion of physical illness stemming from his combat engagements, attributing his mental anguish to the horrors he witnessed.

Sensing the Emperor's reluctance to seek medical help, the Queen proposed seeking solace from the royal priest, *Raja Purohita,* whose *puranic* explanations and justifications could comfort his troubled mind.

The Emperor remained silent, prompting the Queen to realize that perhaps solace needed to come from her support and encouragement. Despite their lack of intimate confidences over the years, she resolved to try, knowing that sometimes, even the most stubborn rulers needed someone to confide in and offer solace.

The Queen could feel during his silence that he expected solace from her. She should give him mental support and courage when he was bent down with impatience and agony. That was not expected from the royal priest. She felt that since their marriage, the Emperor had not been allowed to confide in and listen to her; he was allergic to soft words, beauty, and amusement. He only knew how to impose his ideas and dominated verbal communication, so much so that decades have passed only listening to his advice. He never lends his ears to anybody. But as she got a chance, let her try.

The Chief Queen found herself grappling with the task of comforting the Emperor, a situation unfamiliar to her as she was not accustomed to sympathizing with others in distress. Nevertheless she endeavoured to understand the root of the Emperor's current state of mind. She instructed Ganga to Summon Sumanta, the horse carriage coachman, to meet her immediately.

Sumanta arrived in no time and bent his back forward in reverence to the Queen before she scrabbled around her inquiry.

"Sumanta, can you shed light on the Emperor's troubles? Despite his victory in the Great War, he appears gloomy, lonely, and withdrawn. What could be causing his distress?" she inquired with curiosity.

"The matter is complex, Your Majesty. Any conqueror faced with such a battle would likely experience turmoil," Sumanta explained solemnly.

The Queen's curiosity piqued further as she pressed for details. "But was it not a clear victory? What occurred after the battle?" she asked.

Sumanta's pause was brief, but it was enough to covey the weight of his words. "Yes, it was a victory. But the regiments from Ujjain of Avantiratha and Takshashila of Uttarapatha, in their wake, left a trail of significant collateral damage. The devastation was so extensive that it seemed to awaken a deity of Kalinga from its slumber, confronting our Emperor with the harsh reality of our actions. Unfortunately, our return route was destined to pass through these areas of destruction, exposing us to the grim aftermath. The Emperor, burdened by the sight of such atrocities, was plunged into a state of remorse and mental instability. This is a situation that demands our utmost precision."

Sumanta offered a unique perspective on the turmoil plaguing the victorious ruler as the coachman who witnessed the Emperor's anguish.

The Chief Queen recognized the gravity of the situation. A physical or mental stimulus did not afflict the Emperor; instead, he faced a spiritual curse that threatened his well-being. The coachman's story, involving a deity from the battlefield's graveyard, indicated a dangerous predicament. Graveyard deities were known to be formidable entities, and if one incurred their curse, it was believed that no remedy could save him.

Determined to find a solution for the Emperor's affliction, the Chief Queen devised a plan. She decided to seek the counsel of the royal priest, who she believed would possess the knowledge and expertise to address spiritual matters. She instructed Ganga to summon the priest.

She hoped the priest would guide her in alleviating the Emperor's suffering immediately. The priest, already present among the crowd gathered to celebrate the Emperor's victory, approached the Queen to inquire about the troubling issue.

"It is not my victor that troubles me, Rajaguru," the Emperor began solemnly. "I am haunted by ghastly scenes that assail my conscience relentlessly. A tall Kalinga woman, whose spirit seems to linger from the battlefield, torments me incessantly. No royal physician can offer me relief. With your knowledge of enchantment and spiritual matters can you protect me from her grasp?"

The priest contemplated the Emperor's plight, recognizing the severity of the situation. After reflection, he responded, "As priests, we deal with gods and deities, but evil spirits of graveyards are beyond our expertise. Only local exorcists, well-versed in the ways of such entities, may possess the means to drive them away."

Despite the jubilant atmosphere surrounding Pataliputra's celebration of the Kalinga victory, a sense of disappointment lingered as the Emperor's affliction remained unresolved, leaving those around him feeling helpless in the face of his suffering.

The Chief Queen, deeply concerned about the Emperor's condition, recognized the urgency of seeking help beyond the palace walls. She turned to trusted royal advisors like Mukhya Amat, Radhagupta, who had previously proved himself a valuable ally.

When informed of the Emperor's plight, Radhagupta swiftly joined the Chief Queen, expressing genuine sympathy. Understanding the severity of the Emperor's affliction, he proposed a practical solution.

"We must seek out a spiritual healer from the local area and consult him first," Radhagupta suggested. "The prospect of finding a *tantrika* or exorcist from Kalinga may be slim, given the current circumstances in the aftermath of the war. However, the *tantrikas* from Toshali and its surroundings might have experienced dealing with entities such as the graveyard deity troubling the Emperor. We need to find a way to locate them."

The Chief Amat grasped the gravity of the situation. The Emperor's distress stemmed from his profound responsibility for the war's consequences. As long as he carried this burden, no external remedy could alleviate his suffering. The solution, therefore, lay in finding someone from Kalinga who could empathize with his experience and provide the necessary understanding and comfort.

Given the current circumstances, identifying a resident of Kalinga, particularly one from Toshali, posed a challenge. However, Radhagupta took it upon himself to locate the best spiritual healers in the area, ensuring that three top-tier spirit enchanters were brought forward to assist the Emperor.

Radhagupta, the chief minister, was fully aware of the Kalinga situation. He disapproved of the Emperor's camp at the Toshali hillside battlefield in Kalinga and his commanding the battle at the forefront. Even if he had fought on the occasion, he should have left as soon as the war ended.

As the days passed without any success in removing the spirit that tormented the Emperor, desperation grew within the palace walls. Each attempt by local healers and *tantrikas* failed to alleviate the Emperor's suffering, leaving the situation increasing dire. The presence of the possessing spirit seemed to linger stubbornly, defying all conventional exorcism methods.

The healers suggested that only a Kalinga *tantrika,* familiar with the nuances of the spirit world in the aftermath of the Kalinga War, could address the Emperor's condition. However, the prospect of finding such *tantrika* seemed remote and uncertain, given the tumultuous state of Kalinga and Toshali post-war.

The *Mukhya Amat*, Radhagupta, faced with the Emperor's deteriorating condition, grappled with the grim reality before him. Despite his efforts to explore alternatives, no viable solution could be found. With each passing day, the Emperor's health declined, weighing down his spirit with the burden of his anguish.

In the dire moment, Radhagupta recognized that his only hope lay with Karuvaki, the Emperor's Queen Consort, a resident of Kaushambi palace and her baby boy, Tival. Despite their distance, he knew Karuvaki was resilient and determined to confront the challenges ahead. He conveyed the gravity of the situation without hesitation and sent her an urgent message, urging her to return to the capital immediately.

Karuvaki, unaware of the extent of her husband's suffering, received the summon from Radhagupta with a sense of urgency. Realizing the gravity of the situation, she instantly prepared herself to reach the capital, her heart heavy with concern for the Emperor's well-being. As she embarked on the journey back to Pataliputra, she braced herself for the daunting task that lay ahead, determined to do whatever it took to save her husband from the clutches of the evil spirit that threatened to consume him.

Mukhya Amat's concern for Emperor Piyadasi Raja Ashoka's well-being weighed heavily on his mind. As he contemplated the root cause of the Emperor's distress following the Kalinga War, he grappled with the moral and ethical implications of the post-war devastation inflicted upon the people of Kalinga and the Kalinga soil. Despite the victory achieved on the battlefield, *Mukhya Amat* could not reconcile the indiscriminate destruction wrought upon Kalinga with the principles of righteousness and compassion espoused by the Emperor.

In his relentless pursuit of easing the Emperor's mental anguish and desolation, *Mukhya Amat* contemplated seeking solace and guidance from the local deities. He was very well aware of the Emperor's vulnerability and deep-rooted belief in Buddhist principles of *Ahimsa* and reverence for life. *Mukhya Amat* pondered the potential of Hindu deities, Jain temples and Buddhist *Sanghas* to offer comfort and healing to the Emperor, whose inner turmoil seemed insurmountable.

He also felt guilty for what the Emperor had done. The Emperor was almost a lay Buddhist, aware of the Buddhist principle of *Ahimsa* and pity of life. He was bewildered by the atrocious cruelty committed by the Magadha army even after the battle was won.

Yet, *Mukhya Amat* hesitated to take action, waiting for the arrival of Queen Karuvaki. He believed that her presence would bring much-needed stability and support to the Emperor during his time of need. He understood her pivotal role she would play in accompanying the Emperor through his recovery journey, trusting that her wisdom and compassion would lead him towards healing and redemption.

In the meantime, *Mukhya Amat* remained vigilant, ready to implement whatever measures were necessary to aid the Emperor in overcoming his affliction and restoring peace to the kingdom. As he awaited Queen Karuvaki's return, he contemplated the complexities of the Emperor's suffering and its intricate web of spiritual and moral considerations

As the day drew to a close and the sun dipped below the western horizon, signalling the end of their with the rock elephant, Budu and Kalu were reluctant to take leave and depart. Despite the passing of time, their eagerness to hear more stories lingered, holding them captive in the presence of the ancient stone elephant.

Gazing at the unmoving face of the rock elephant, they felt a sense of connection to the unseen and unbelievable tales of the Dark Ages. In their minds, history was not merely a record of facts and figures but a tapestry woven from literature, folktales, and the imagination. They saw themselves as chosen vessels destined to uncover the hidden truths buried in the oblivion of the past.

Despite the fading light due to the shadows of nearby trees, Budu and Kalu remained rooted to the spot, unwilling to let go of the opportunity to delve deeper into the mysteries of the past. For them, the stories whispered by the rock elephant held the promise of enlightenment and understanding, drawing them ever closed to the elusive secrets of history. And as they stood in silent reverence before the ancient artifact, they knew their journey was far from over, for the mysteries of the ages stretched out before them, waiting to be explored.

[Piyadasi]

Karuvaki in Kaushambi Palace –

Kalu and Budu, two avid listeners, became increasingly engrossed in the historical narrative unfolding before them. Despite the grim nature of the events they heard about, they couldn't help but feel a deep sense of sorrow and empathy for their forefathers who had suffered at the hands of the remorseless Emperor of Magadha, Ashoka the Black, a ruler whose name was etched in the annals of their ancestral homeland millennia ago.

While they harboured no pity for the Emperor, who had inflicted such pain and suffering upon their ancestors, they found a strange satisfaction in witnessing his torment and remorse in the aftermath of the war. Each moment of his agony brought them a sense of vindication as if the suffering he endured was a form of cosmic justice for the atrocities he had committed.

Despite the depressing nature of the subject matter, Kalu and Budu were filled with eager anticipation for the next installment of the story. They hastened their steps towards the rock elephant, their excitement mounting with each stride. Upon reaching their destination, they paid their respects to the divine presence within the rock, feeling a sense of reverence and thrill as they prepared to hear the next chapter in the saga of the Magadha Emperor.

The scene was set in Kaushambi, the bustling capital of the Vatsa Janapada, nestled along the left bank of the

Yamuna River in the heart of *Madhyadesha*, India. This ancient city served as a pivotal hub for trade, boasting convenient land and river routes that facilitated transportation via chariots, animal-driven carts, and large boats.

From its centre, four wide roads spanned out in each cardinal direction = East, West, North, and South – providing easy access to and from the city. Kaushambi's rich history intertwined with the ebb and flow of the Yamuna, each ripple echoing the tale of its heritage. Legend had it that the city derived its name from the third son of Uparichara Manu, a figure steeped in the lore of the Mahabharata, tracing its roots back to the epochs of the Dwapara Yuga.

Through the ages, Kaushambi had witnessed the reign of numerous dynasties, but it truly flourished under the Mauryas. Chandragupta Maurya, the dynasty's founder, established a palace within the city's confines, capitalizing on its strategic location within his burgeoning empire. However, his grandson, the illustrated Emperor Piyadasi Ashoka, truly fell under the city's spell.

During Ashoka's reign, Kaushambi experienced a renaissance of sorts. The Mauryan palaces and administrative buildings, once vulnerable to termite infestation due to their wooden structure, were now transformed into formidable stone edifices. Skilled stone sculptors adorned the plan walls with intricate architectural designs, ushering in an era of stone craftsmanship that originated in the Western realms.

The foreign queen of Chandragupta Maurya—Helena partly influenced this architectural shift. Hailing from the Seleucid Kingdom, where the use of stone in construction and art was rapidly evolving, Helena's background likely played a significant role in introducing and promoting stone-based architecture within the Maurya Empire, particularly in the burgeoning city of Kaushambi.

As thesun cast its warm glow over the city of Kaushambi, the queen, adorned in regal attire, surveyed her domain from the palace's balcony. From this vantage point, she could see the bustling streets below, alive with the vibrant comings and goings of merchants, artisans, and common folk, each adding their unique energy to the city's pulse.

Kaushambi, under the Maurya rule, flourished and earned its status as a sub-capital or second capital of the empire during the reign of Piyadasi Raja, the third-generation Emperor. This elevation was not without reason. Kaushambi, strategically located along the Yamuna River, offered significant advantages. It was a bustling trade hub and a centre of religious activity, its importance echoing through the ages.

Piyadasi Raja, proud of his heritage and enthusiastic about modernity, took great interest in the development of Kaushambi. The palace, overlooking the river, underwent extensive renovations, symbolizing the Maurya dynasty's prosperity and cultural refinement. Its walls were adorned with exquisite Gandhar art, showcasing the empire's artistic prowess.

From the palace's balconies, one could witness the picturesque sight of boats gliding along the Yamuna, laden with agricultural and forest produce. The river, teeming with activity, reflected the vibrant energy of Kaushambi's commercial endeavour. However, amidst the hustle and bustle of trade, the serenity of the natural scenery often went unnoticed by the buy merchants, their minds preoccupied with the demands of commerce.

Yet, for those fortunate enough to pause and admire the view, the sight of geese gracefully playing in the rippling waters offered a serene and peaceful moment, a stark contrast to the bustling activity of Kaushambi's riverfront.

The palace is a focal point of attraction for some northern observers who ascend boats along the Yamuna. Among them is Queen Karuvaki, the favoured consort of the third Maurya Emperor, who has chosen to reside here rather than in the capital palace of Pataliputra. Despite being the second Queen, Karuvaki holds a prominent position as the Queen Consort and enjoys freedom afforded by her husband's preference for Kaushambi.

Accompanying Queen Karuvaki is her young son, Tivara, who is known for his keen observation and thoughtful demeanour at the age of eight. He often poses numerous questions, reflecting his curious nature and inquisitive mind.

Subodha, the Chamberlain of Pataliputra, arrived at the palace during the midday sun, suggesting the urgency of his visit. Bowing responsibility at the queen's feet per royal custom, Subodha acknowledge the summer importance of his message.

"Your Majesty, Rani Maa, I bring my respects," Subodha begins, addressing the queen. "Indeed, my journey has been swift, prompted by urgent matters that require your attention. There are developments of significance that I must relay to you without delay."

Queen Karuvaki, sensing the gravity of the situation, prepares to receive the news with a mix of apprehension and determination.

"My regards, Your Majesty, Rani Maa," greeted Subodha, bowing respectfully at the queen's feet, adhering to the customs of the royal court.

"Welcome, Subodha! Your arrival at this hour after such a long absence piqued my curiosity. Your haste suggests urgency. Did you embark on your journey during the evening hours? Do you carry news of importance?" inquired the Queen, her apprehension evident in her voice.

"Rani Maa, Maharaja has just returned from the Kalinga War victorious," said Pratihara Subodha taking seat on the floor as customary.

The Queen's expression shifted to one of astonishment. "What has happened? Is he unwell physically?" she enquired.

"Physically, he is fine," replied Subodha, "but he is completely broken, to the point of being bedridden. It starkly contrasts to our typical energetic and steadfast Piyadasi Ashoka."

The Queen pondered this revelation. "But how can this be? The victory in Kalinga would typically be cause for great celebration among the people of Magadha. How could Maharaja withdraw himself from such an occasion?"

Subodha shook his head. "The victory ceremony has not yet taken place in Pataliputra. Despite the cheers and slogans echoing, the palace remains silent, with the ailing Emperor at its centre."

"I am bewildered, Subodha. Why does the Emperor not revel in the triumph he vehemently pursued? Despite all the obstacles and inhibitions, he unleashed his wrath upon Kalinga. What has prevented him from relishing the long-awaited victory and its accompanying joy?" Karuvaki questioned, reflecting on her confusion and concern.

Subodha sighed deeply, understanding the queen's distress. "Something unfortunate has occurred. When the Emperor returned from Kalinga to Magadha, he withdrew into himself, muttering deliriously about '*Adhamma*', '*Adhamma*'; '*Dhamma*' and '*Dhamma*'. He sits in a brooding posture as if burdened by an unpardonable misdeed. He is oblivious to his surroundings and unable to respond to any inquiries. It's as though he is consumed by deep remorse. It is a perplexing state for such a powerful Emperor, a towering figure in the Maurya Empire, whose achievements include countless captives and a mass slaughter numbering in thousands. Yet, despite these triumphs, he is haunted by a profound darkness," explained the Pratihara, his voice resonating with conviction.

Karuvaki pondered deeply, reluctant to divulge even a single word of her introspection, which probed into the inner workings of the Maurya family's fame and secrets.

She struggled to comprehend what could have transpired after the victory in Kalinga. Throughout their twelve years of marital life, she had observed her husband in every conceivable situation. She knew him intimately, understood his character, and always regarded him as a man of little sympathy and rarely forgiving. How could he be so profoundly affected by what should have been a triumphant victory? How could a man who had witnessed the death of many of his brothers with seemingly no emotional response, like a heartless stone statue, suddenly be so overcome with anguish at the loss of a kingdom and its subjects united in defence of their homeland? Karuvaki searched tirelessly for the root causes of her husband's sorrow.

As a daughter of Kalinga, Karuvaki couldn't help but feel betrayed by her husband's actions. She reminded him of his acceptance of her, a Kalinga princess, into his life and kingdom, acknowledging Kalinga as her rightful homeland.

But now, reflecting on the events unfolding, she couldn't shake the feeling of overwhelming Magadha imperialism, crushing Kalinga beneath its weight. Kalinga had never posed a threat or committed any wrongdoing to warrant such aggression. She recalled a story her grandmother used to tell, the tale of the Tiger and the Kid. In the story, the Tiger upstream accused the Kid of polluting the water he drank from, only to realize the hypocrisy of his accusation when confronted with the truth. It was a metaphor for unjust accusations and double standards Karuvaki saw parallels between this story and the relationship between Magadha and Kalinga – accusations made to justify aggression and domination.

As Queen Karuvaki grappled with the conflicting emotions stirred within her, she couldn't shake the nagging doubt that her people much like the bold Kid in the story, were unfairly accused and persecuted by the mighty Magadha Empire. The tales passed down by her grandmother echoed in her mind, painting a vivid picture of the suffering endured by her homeland at the hands of her husband's actions. Despite this turmoil, she found solace in the care and confidence bestowed upon her by the Emperor, a comfort that she held tightly amidst the chaos.

Settled in the renovated Kaushambi palace, Karuvaki and her small child found themselves amidst the hustle and bustle of royal life, surrounded by a second set of royal attendants. The palace, once a hub of trade and culture, now buzzed with activity, starkly contrasting the quieter days spent in the Lalitagiri settlement.

Karuvaki knew of the tensions between Magadha and Kalinga, her ancestral homeland. Having grown up under the protection of her father, a vassal king of Kalinga, she understood the intricate web of politics and power dynamics at play. Her father's wealth and influence as a prominent maritime merchant had shielded her from much of the strife that plagued the region.

However, when news of the sudden outbreak of war reached her, Karuvaki's world was turned upside down. The conflict between Kalinga and Magadha once confined to border skirmishes and diplomatic negotiations, had erupted into a full-blown war, leaving her feeling helpless and betrayed.

As she heard of her husband's illness, the victorious king who had led the charge against her people, Karuvaki felt a surge of shock and concern. Without hesitation, she made preparations to journey to Pataliputra, the heart of the Magadha Empire, determined to confront the truth and seek answers to the questions that plagued her mind.

As the day's tale drew close, the two attentive listeners grappled with the revelation that astounded them. The realization that Queen Karuvaki, the beloved wife of Emperor Piyadasi, was none other than the proud princess of Kalinga added a new layer of complexity to the story. Here was a woman deeply connected to both sides of the conflict, bound by blood ties and allegiance to her homeland, yet also wedded to the very ruler who had let the devastating war against her kith and kin. Her inner conflict, a battle of loyalty and love, was poignant of the human cost of war.

The irony of Karuvaki's situation struck a chord with the listeners as they pondered the unfortunate twist of fate that had led to such a tragic turn of events. To think that Kalinga, with Karuvaki as its proud princes, had unwittingly become embroiled in a conflict under the command of her husband, the Emperor, was a bitter pill to swallow.

As they went home, their minds buzzed with a newfound perplexity. The weight of the day's revelations hung heavy, stirring up conflicting emotions. What had begun as a simple quest for knowledge had morphed into a profound exploration of human nature, fate, and the tangled webs of history.

They could no longer view the war and its aftermath through lenses of detached curiosity. Now, with the knowledge of Karuvaki's connection to both sides of the conflict, they felt a deep sense of empathy and sorrow for the suffering endured by all involved. The once-distant tale had become uncomfortably close, forcing them to confront the harsh realities of war and its far-reaching consequences.

[Kasaumbi Pillar]

Drowning into Unfathomable Depth of Remorse

Kalu and Budu, deeply immersed in the historical context of Emperor Ashoka and the Kalinga War, couldn't shake off the restlessness that had settled upon them. Their minds buzzed with doubts and questions about the nature of humanity, especially when viewed through the lens of power and royalty. They grappled with the notion that Kings and Emperors, with their lofty titles and grandeur, could so callously disregard the lives and well-being of ordinary people, even close to them.

As they made their way to the rock elephant, their steps were heavy with contemplation. They couldn't fathom how a King, especially one with marital ties to a kingdom, could orchestrate a devastating war against his beloved Queen's motherland. It seemed like a betrayal of the most profound king, one that defied simple logic and reason.

Yet, they understood that the complexities of history often defied easy explanation. Kings and Emperors, driven by ambition, pride and the pursuit of power, sometimes made incomprehensible decisions to those outside their inner circle. They wielded authority with impunity, often disregarding the human cost of their actions in favour of their glory and legacy. 3

Arriving at the rock elephant, they eagerly awaited

the continuation of the tale, hoping to glean further insights into the enigmatic figure of Emperor Piyadasi and the tumultuous events of his reign. The rock elephant held the key to unlocking the mysteries of the past, shedding light on the motivations and machinations of those who shaped history with their actions. With patient ears and open minds, they prepared to delve deeper into the secrets of the ancient world.

The rock elephant continued his tale .....

As the sun set over the ancient capital of Pataliputra, a heavy cloud of silence hung over the palace of Emperor Piyadasi. The air, thick with the weight of remorse, seemed to suffocate even the most stubborn hearts. Victory had been achieved on the battlefield, yet it brought no joy to the conqueror's soul.

Emperor Piyadasi, once the mighty ruler of the Maurya Empire, now sat alone in his chambers, his mind a turbulent sea of regret and sorrow. The cheers of his soldiers, the cries of the vanquished, and the blood-soaked fields of Kalinga haunted him relentlessly. The once proud warrior now found himself shackled by the chains of remorse, a depressive state of his being that profoundly affected his wives and the entire palace.

Amidst the solemn atmosphere of the palace, the Chief Queen, adorned in regal attire, stood firmly by her husband's side, her heart heavy with concern. She had witnessed the Emperor's transformation, his spirit broken by the horrors of war. Despite her efforts to comfort him, his grief seemed impenetrable. Her steadfastness in such despair was a testament to her love and loyalty.

It was then that the second Queen, Karuvaki, arrived from the distant palace of Kaushambi; her presence was a candle of hope amidst the darkness. Sensing the depth of her husband's anguish, she implored him to seek solace beyond the walls of Pataliputra, to find respite in the tranquil embrace of nature. Her love and compassion for the Emperor were the guiding lights in this dark period of their lives.

Karuvaki's decision to relocate the remorseful Emperor from the palace in Pataliputra to Kaushambi sparked a glimmer of hope within the royal family. Radhagupta recognized the potential benefits of this move, believing that a change in environment could help alleviate the Emperor's deepening mental anguish and provide him with a sense of solace.

Before any further plans could be made, Radhagupta approached Karuvaki with a proposal to address the Emperor's gloom. He suggested seeking the blessings of the local deities of Pataliputra, underlining their longstanding presence and revered status within the city. The deities, known for their benevolence and power, were believed to bring relief to the Emperor and help restore his well-being.

In agreement with Radhagupta's proposal, Karuvaki acknowledged the importance of involving the blessings of Lord Shiva, Deity Parvati and other deities worshipped in Pataliputra. She emphasized the need for proper worship and offerings to all the Gods and Goddesses in the vicinity, expressing her belief that their divine intervention could aid the Emperor's recovery.

With a renewed sense of relief and determination, Karuvaki and Radhagupta pledged to embark on a journey of spiritual devotion, seeking the blessings of the local deities to alleviate the Emperor's suffering and guide him back to normalcy. Their unshakeable faith in divine intervention infused hope and optimism in their quest to restore health to the Emperor and peace to the kingdom.

The Emperor's vow to pursue peace and enlightenment was a beacon of hope in such dark times.

The worship of Lord Shiva in the temple at Pataliputra stirred anticipation among people, who believed that the Emperor would soon recover from his affliction with the deity's blessings. Karuvaki, accompanying the Emperor, participated in the grand ritual held at the temple. The air was filled with the scent of incense and chanting, creating a sacred atmosphere. Lord Shiva was enthusiastically venerated; he was adorned with a serpent around his neck and was clad in the traditional attire mentioned in the Vedas.

Despite the priest's assurances that the Emperor would recover soon from his mental anguish, days passed without any noticeable change in his demeanour. He remained listless and detached from the world around him, his mind still plagued by deep-seated fears. The Emperor's faith in the Hindu deities waned as he questioned why they had not warned him about the horrors of war, leading him to revisit his decision on the conquest of Kalinga. His internal struggle and questioning of the deities were a testament to his deep emotional turmoil and thirst for the spiritual journey.

Disappointed by no divine intervention, the Emperor harboured suspicions towards Lord Shiva, doubting whether the deity had punished him for his moral transgressions. His doubts about the deities and his disappointment at their perceived non-intervention were a significant part of his emotional journey.

Despite the elaborate worship conducted by the most esteemed Purohita, the Emperor found no solace in the temple rituals, further deepening his disillusionment and uncertainty.

As the weekend approached, Queen Karuvaki found no improvement in her husband's condition, prompting her to seek solace from the Gaon Devati of Patali, a revered deity known for granting the wishes of her devotees. Accompanied by royal assistants bearing offerings of red flowers, the Queen performed an elaborate worship ceremony to obtain assurance of the Emperor's recovery.

However, as the Emperor observed the vibrant red hibiscus flowers offered to the Goddess, he couldn't shake the feeling that they could never appease her. Red, reminiscent of the blood-soaked battlefield and Daya River beside Toshali in Kalinga only intensified his guilt and fear. Despite the earnest prayers and offerings for the Emperor's recovery, he remained trapped in his turmoil, unnoticed by all, including the Queen. His feelings of guilt and fear were overwhelming, which painted a vivid picture of turbulent state of his being.

Despite the true-hearted worship and the abundance of offerings, the deity remained unmoved by the pleas for the Emperor's well-being. It was as if a dark presence from Kalinga, too potent for even the protective forces of the local deity to overcome, had accompanied the Emperor. The Emperor's fate seemed to hand in the balance, his recovery uncertain.

Karuvaki was deeply troubled by the lack of results from their worship efforts. Even the priests admitted that the Emperor's sins might have outweighed the blessings bestowed upon him by the heavens. Determined to understand the situation fully, she approached the Emperor directly to inquire about the events on the Kalinga battlefield and her actions in detail – his attire, hairstyle, and how she vanished from his sight only to reappear in his dreams and haunting visions.

The Emperor could only provide vague recollections of the events, insisting that the statuesque of Kalinga had not wrongly accused him. He described the figure not as an ordinary woman but as a manifestation of his guilt and remorse – a natural obsession of the mind haunting him relentlessly. Trapped by his sense of morality and humanity, he saw the Kalinga deity as a fitting punishment for his atrocious actions.

Realizing that staying in the Pataliputra palace would not change the Emperor's condition, Karuvaki understood that they needed to alter his environment to alter his mindset. Her unwavering determination and belief in the power of change were necessary to guide him towards healing and recovery. Firm persuasion and motivation were essential to guide him towards healing and recovery.

With a heavy heart, Emperor Ashoka acquiesced to his second wife's suggestion. Together, they embarked on a journey to Kaushambi, a consecrated place that held the promise of erasing the guilt from the battle-ridden mind of the Emperor, who was now chargeable with genocide. Surrounded by the serene beauty of the countryside, the Emperor found a momentary reprieve from the burden of his sorrows.

Yet, even amidst Kaushambi's tranquillity, Ashoka's mind remained tormented by memories of the recent past. Restless wanderings consumed his days, and his nights were plagued by haunted dreams. No temple could offer absolution, and no prayer could quell the storm raging within his soul.

Karuvaki stood steadfast by her husband's side as the weeks turned into months, her unwavering devotion as the lamp of hope lighted in the darkest times. With gentle words and tender gestures, she sought to soothe the

Emperor's troubled heart, to remind him of the love and compassion that still existed in the world.

And slowly, ever so slowly, the walls of remorse began to crumble, replaced by a glimmer of hope and redemption. Emperor Ashoka, once consumed by grief, now found solace in the embrace of his beloved wife in the quiet moments shared beneath the starlit sky.

Though the scars of war would forever mark his soul, Ashoka emerged a changed man from the shadows of his remorse. Inspired by the compassion and understanding of his second Queen, he vowed to dedicate his life to the pursuit of peace and enlightenment to ensure that the atrocities of war would never again darken the lands of his empire.

So, guided by the gentle wisdom of Karuvaki, Emperor Ashoka embarked on a new journey, one filled with hope, forgiveness, and the promise of a brighter tomorrow. As he looked towards the horizon, he knew that anything could be possible with his beloved Queen by his side.

The day's story was over, apparently brief compared to earlier episodes. Both the guys stood up and left the place after praying to the rock elephant.

Kalu and Budu couldn't shake off the restlessness that had settled upon them after hearing the unsettling tale of Karuvaki and the Kalinga War. Their minds buzzed with doubts and questions about the nature of humanity, especially when viewed through the lens of power and royalty. They grappled with the notion that Kings and Emperors, with their lofty titles and grandeur, could so callously disregard the lives and well-being of ordinary people, even those close to them.

As they made their way out of the rock elephant, their minds were heavy with contemplation. They couldn't fathom how a king, especially one with marital ties to a kingdom, could orchestrate a devastating war against his wife's motherland. It seemed like a betrayal of the most profound, one that defied simple logic and reason.

Yet, they understood that the complexities of history often defied easy explanation. Kings and Emperors, driven by ambition, pride, and the pursuit of power, sometimes made incomprehensible decisions to those outside their inner circle. They wielded authority with impunity, often disregarding the human cost of their actions in favour of their glory and legacy. 3

Arriving at the rock elephant, they eagerly awaited the continuation of the tale, hoping to glean further insight into the enigmatic figure of Emperor Piyadasi and the tumultuous events of his reign. The rock elephant held the key to unlocking the mysteries of the past, shedding light on the motivations and machinations of those who shaped history with their actions. With patient ears and open minds, they prepared to dig deeper into the secrets of the ancient world.

Karuvaki's Probe into Guilt and the Remorse

This time, something interesting would be there for Kalu and Budu to listen to. They are expectant that something magical will happen in the place where Karuvaki resided and the Emperor frequently inhabited. No doubt Kaushambi was his favourite place.

Eagerly, Kalu and Budu walked to the rock elephant and worshipped it with all their devotion.

The rock elephant, a majestic symbol of the land's ancient wisdom, welcomed them with a silent nod as if thanking them for their patient hearing. It did not delay in whispering the remaining portion of the story, its voice echoing through the sacred air.

Upon arriving at Kaushambi with Karuvaki, Ashoka was accompanied by attendants and domestic assistants, some of whom possessed nursing skills and knowledge of Ayurvedic principles.

Karuvaki observed a slight improvement in the Emperor's alertness as they settled into their new surroundings. However, his demeanour remained shrouded in gloom, and he remained reticent, offering no voluntary statements.

Karuvaki surmised that the events of the Kalinga War continued to torment his mind, preventing him from finding solace and peace. She understood her husband's character well, recognizing his inherent arrogance and unwavering nature. While Kalinga itself was not unfamiliar to him, the war's profound impact had turned him into his adversary, consumed by guilt and remorse that gnawed at his conscience.

Believing that identifying and addressing the specific events weighing on his mind was essential for his recovery, Karuvaki sought out Sumanta, the coachman who had accompanied the Emperor from Kalinga to the capital, Pataliputra. However, Sumanta was not present in Kaushambi then, prompting Karuvaki to dispatch a team to locate and bring him back from wherever he was. In the meantime, Karuvaki gently inquired about the Emperor's impressions of Kaushambi, hoping to engage him in conversation and glean insight into his mind. The Emperor acknowledged noticing the changes in their new surroundings but confessed to feeling disconnected, unable to derive meaning from his observations.

This response puzzled Karuvaki, who realized the delicate state of the Emperor's mind and resolved not to press him further, fearing it might exacerbate his distress.

The Queen's curiosity about the event surrounding the Emperor's mental distress prompted her to seek information from Sumanta and the two bodyguards who accompanied the Emperor at the Toshali battlefield.

Summoned to a secluded chamber in the northern part of the palace, Sumanta and the bodyguards prepared to discuss matters of great concern to the royal family and the kingdom. After exchanging pleasantries and introductions, the Queen directed her inquiries towards the bodyguards, eager to learn about their experiences during the fall of Kalinga.

"We were indeed present with His Highness during the fall of Kalinga," began *Anta Vashika,* the Chief of Bodyguards of Magadha.

"The toll was immense, and the atmosphere was fraught with tension. Suddenly, His Highness became restless, and we noticed sweat on his forehead. During this time, we observed some spies from Magadha approaching him, bearing news that deeply troubled the Emperor."

[Emperor and Queen]

The Queen listened intently, her curiosity piqued by the mention of the spies and their revelations. "Can you recall any specifics about the information these spies conveyed to the Emperor?" she inquired, hoping to uncover any details that might shed light on the cause of his distress.

Karuvaki listened intently to the account provided by the *Anta Vashika,* feeling a sense of horror wash over her as she grappled with the implications of the Emperor's encounter. The thought of her husband being deeply affected by an unknown force that seemed to transcend the realm of the ordinary filled her with trepidation. She couldn't shake the dread that settled in her stomach as she pondered the mysterious events unfolding around them.

The bodyguard's narrative transported Karuvaki to the battlefield, its grim aftermath vividly painted in her mind. The wounded's cries and the chaos of the war reverberated in her thoughts as she tried to envision the scene that had unfolded before her husband. The sudden appearance of the enigmatic woman, her desperate pleas, and the unanswered questions that hung in the air all contributed to the heavy atmosphere of unease.

As the bodyguard recounted the details of the encounter, Karuvaki's thoughts raced, trying to make sense of the inexplicable. Could this woman be a mere mortal, overcome with grief at the loss of her family, or was she something more, a manifestation of a more profound, more primal force? The notion that supernatural beings might have orchestrated the encounter sent a shiver down her spine, reminding her of the mysteries and dangers that lurked beyond human understanding.

Lost in her thoughts, Karuvaki was overcome by a creeping sense of hopelessness. The realization that even the Emperor was powerless against these otherworldly forces weighed heavily on her. The burden of responsibility bore down on her, the daunting task of finding a solution to her husband's affliction seeming insurmountable. With each passing moment, the path ahead appeared more treacherous than she had ever anticipated.

Karuvaki listened attentively to the coachman's account, her mind swirling with concern and dread. The mention of the deity in Toshali sent a chill down her spine as she contemplated the possibility of supernatural intervention in her husband's affliction. She knew of the deity's presence in the graveyard near the riverside village and her reputation as a powerful but generally benevolent force in the region. Yet, her displeasure towards the Emperor filled Karuvaki with a sense of foreboding.

Karuvaki couldn't shake the unease over her as she considered the coachman's words. The image of her husband, sleepless and muttering incoherently during their journey, weighed heavily on her mind. It was clear that something had deeply unsettled him, something beyond mortal comprehension.

The coachman's description of the journey only served to deepen Karuvaki's sense of unease. The war-ravaged villages they encountered along the way, the widows and orphans left in the wake of the conflict, painted a grim picture of the devastation wrought by the Emperor's campaign. The sight of the Jain pious centre, its monks brutally murdered, added another layer of sorrow and despair to the already sad journey.

As Karuvaki sat in contemplation, her thoughts turned to the events that had unfolded before them. She couldn't shake the feeling that their journey had been guided by unseen forces beyond their control or understanding. The notion that they had been led to witness the aftermath of the Emperor's actions filled her with profound sorrow and guilt.

Deep in thought, Karuvaki couldn't help but wonder what role these events might play in her husband's recovery. If some higher power orchestrated them, what would it mean for their future?

The weight of responsibility pressed down on her shoulders as she grappled with the implications of their journey, knowing that the path ahead would be fraught with uncertainty and danger.

Karuvaki's desperate hope that the Emperor's relocation from Pataliputra to Kaushambi would bring him solace was shattered. Despite the change in scenery, her husband's depression only deepened, leaving her to watch in anguish as he retreated further from the world. His apathy, detachment, and isolation pained her deeply, stirring a resolve within her to find a way to bring him back.

She realized that the source of his affliction was not a simple matter of minor gloom but something far more sinister and inexplicable. The supernatural force that had taken hold of him was not easily removed, especially considering its origins in the blood-soaked fields of Kalinga. Karuvaki knew all too well the power of such forces, having witnessed the exorcisms and rituals performed in the villages of her homeland.

She considered seeking help from a healer in the northwest villages of Toshali, where the deity *Smasanadevi* was said to reside. However, she knew the practical challenges of such a task and felt hopeless about finding a solution post-war in such remote and dangerous territory.

Turning her thoughts to other avenues, Karuvaki considered consulting the royal priest at Kaushambi despite the failure of the previous attempt by the priest of Pataliputra there. She wondered if some alternative approach or ritual could be performed to alleviate the Emperor's suffering.

Meanwhile, the kingdom's advisors speculated that the Emperor's condition resulted from a divine curse, perhaps inflicted by one of the Twenty-four Jain *Sasanadevis* associated with the Jain Tirthankaras. This added another layer of complexity to Karuvaki's dilemma as she grappled with the idea of the supernatural in her husband's affliction.

Feeling increasingly perplexed and desperate for answers, Karuvaki decided to take decisive action. She called upon the Chief Intelligence Officer, *Sarpa Mahamatra,* to gather detailed information about the of the Kalinga War and to track down the two mysterious figures dressed in black who had poisoned the Emperor's mind on the battlefield. It was a risky gambit, but Karuvaki knew that she had to uncover the truth behind her husband's suffering if she ever hoped to find a cure.

Sarpa Mahamatra, the Chief Intelligence Officer of the Maurya Empire, was deeply alarmed by the revelation of the two mysterious black-clad spies who had managed to infiltrate the Emperor's camp during the closing days of the monstrous war. These individuals had accessed the Emperor with vital information that seemed to have affected his mental state, leaving *Sarpa Mahamatra* feeling responsible and guilty for failing to prevent such an intrusion.

In response to Queen Karuvaki's plea for answers, *Sarpa Mahamatra* vowed to use the vast and formidable intelligence network of Magadha to track down and apprehend all known spies, whether they were stationary *Sthanikas* or wandering *Sanharas* or any other type of covert operatives.

Queen Karuvaki, hailing from Kalinga herself, was

heartened by *Sarpa Mahamatra*'s resolve and grasp of the situation's severity. The devastation wrought by her husband's military campaigns in her homeland had left her with a profound sense of sorrow and regret. Her marriage to Prince Piyadasi had severed her ties with her family, leaving her feeling estranged from her roots and unaware of the tragic events that had occurred to her people.

The complexities of court intrigue and the rumours surrounding her husband's rise to power were not the focus of Karuvaki's concerns. Her singular obsession was finding a way to restore her husband's shattered mind and bring him back to a state of normalcy.

As *Sarpa Mahamatra* embarked on his mission with unwavering determination, Karuvaki was consumed by the weight of her duties and the urgent need to uncover the truth behind the Emperor's affliction. The path ahead was fraught with peril and uncertainty, but she was resolute in her commitment to preserve for her husband's and the kingdom's sake.

Sarpa Mahamatra's explanation vividly portrayed the complex relationship between Magadha and Kalinga, shedding light on the intricate web of espionage and intelligence operations that had evolved over the decades. Although outwardly composed as he spoke, the Queen was inwardly intrigued by his account, recognizing familiar places and dynamics from her life in Toshali.

"Your Honour, Ma'am," *Sarpa* continued, "the diplomatic landscape between Magadha and Kalinga has changed profoundly. Our intelligence duties in Kalinga date back to the later years of the Founding Maurya Emperor's reign. During the reign of Bindusar, known as *Amitrachates* or *Amitraghata*, our intelligence activities expanded significantly."

Sarpa's recounting of the espionage efforts revealed the extent to which Magadha had penetrated Kalinga's society and governance. Toshali, the capital city of Kalinga, had become a focal point for Magadha's intelligence network, with spies infiltrating all levels of society and government. The local people, unaware of their true intentions, referred to them as the "whispering people", reflecting the clandestine nature of their activities.

The Queen listened intently, her mind filled with memories of her upbringing in Toshali and her father's involvement in the Royal Council of Kalinga at Toshali. She concealed her connection to the subject matter from *Sarpa Mahamatra,* who continued to provide insight into the complexities of Magadha's intelligence operations in Kalinga.

"As our empire expanded", *Sarpa* explained, "we faced challenges in monitoring maritime trade due to our limited access to the sea, primarily confined to a small area along the Ratnakar Bay on the Arabian side. This posed a significant obstacle for our intelligence gathering efforts, as we sought to understand Kalinga's dimension of maritime activities and its administration."

The Queen, absorbed in these details, her thoughts weaving between past and present, her connection to Toshali and her current predicament with the troubled Emperor, remained poised. She was eager to glean any insight that might aid her in exposing the mysteries surrounding the Emperor's condition and the events of the Kalinga War, her determination shining through.

The gathering of Magadha's spies, both local and wandering, in the remote hall of Kaushambi's palace left Queen Karuvaki both intrigued and deeply concerned. She keenly felt the weight of her husband's affliction and understood the necessity of gathering crucial information from these covert operatives to aid in unravelling the mysteries surrounding it.

As *Sarpa Mahamatra* briefed her on the composition of the assembled spies, the Queen's attention focused keenly on the two black-dressed individuals, *Drishya-Adrishya* and *Bhramita,* who had encountered the Emperor on the battlefield. The Chief Intelligence authority explained that these two spied and the other pair clad in white had served as the Emperor's trusted confidants, providing vital information and insights.

However, the absence of the black-clothed spies presumed lost on the outskirts of the battlefield, posed a significant and immediate challenge. Karuvaki realized these missing operatives were not just a puzzle piece but potentially held the key to understanding the events that affected the Emperor's mind.

"Chief Mahamatra," the Queen addressed *Sarpa* with a resolute tone, "We must not rest until we locate these black-attire spies. Their knowledge of the battlefield encounter is not just important but crucial to understanding the affliction that has befallen my husband."

Sarpa nodded in agreement, acknowledging the importance of uncovering the whereabouts of the missing spies. "Your Highness," he responded, "I will mobilize our network to investigate and trace any leads that might shed light on the fate of *Drishya-Adrishya* and *Bhramita.* Their insights could prove invaluable in addressing the Emperor's condition.

With a sense of urgency, the Queen directed the gathered spies to provide any relevant information they possessed about the battlefield encounter and subsequent events. The assembled operatives, accustomed to secrecy and discretion, awaited the Queen's inquiries with a mixture of respect and apprehension.

In the following days, *Sarpa Mahamatra* and his intelligence network worked tirelessly to uncover clues and track down the missing spies. Meanwhile, Queen Karuvaki delved deeper into the complexities of Magadha's espionage operations and the role of these covert agents in the events surrounding the Kalinga war.

As the investigation progressed, the Queen's determination grew, fuelled by her unwavering commitment to restoring her husband's mental well-being and uncovering the truth behind the supernatural forces that had trapped him. The fate of *Drishya-Adrishya* and *Bhramita* remained a central mystery that holds the key to unlocking the Emperor's recovery and resolving the haunting spectre of the Kalinga War.

The Emperor's delirium and his murmured confessions shook Karuvaki to her core. As she listened to his tortured words, she realized the depth of his inner turmoil and the haunting memories of the Kalinga War that plagued his every thought.

In that dimly lit chamber, the Emperor's words reverberated with the burden of guilt and remorse. His conscience, relentlessly pursuing truth and righteousness, condemned his actions on the battlefield. The questions posed by the mysterious statue-like figure that had appeared before him in Kalinga now echoed in his delirious mutterings, a testament to the profound impact of the encounter.

Karuvaki, torn between her husband's suffering and the harsh reality of his mental torment, endeavoured to comfort him. She invoked the principles of statecraft and kingship, the teachings of Vishnugupta and the Sukraniti, which emphasized the duty of a ruler to safeguard and serve his people. Yet, her efforts to reassure him were dwarfed by his unyielding self-condemnation.

The Emperor's admission of imposing revenue dues upon Kalinga and the subsequent brutal aftermath bore down on him. He grappled with the magnitude of his deeds, lamenting his loss of authority and moral standing. The prospect of being despised by the people he had conquered haunted him, a stark reminder of the price of his conquest.

As the Emperor retreated into the depths of his anguish, Karuvaki struggled to find solace in her words. She urged him to embrace his legacy as a mighty Magadha Emperor, yet she sensed the futility of her reassurances in the face of his inner torment. The Emperor's descent into despair marked a profound turning point that threatened to engulf him.

At that moment, Karuvaki realized that her husband's recovery would take a lot of work. The shadows of the past loomed large and Kalinga ghosts bore witness to his turmoil. As she gazed upon the Emperor's weary form, she resolved to seek answers beyond the confines of their palace walls, determined to confront the spectre of Kalinga that haunted him still.

As Karuvaki, the Maurya Queen born in Kalinga, sat in the west-end hall, she was enveloped by the clandestine web of Magadha's intelligence network. Her mind was a storm of conflicting emotions, a testament to her deep connection with her motherland, Kalinga, and the haunting species that plagued her husband. Her heart, however, remained resolute in its quest to understand the conflict that scarred her land.

With their enigmatic aliases and shadowy personas, the spied unravelled tales of espionage and intrigue that spanned generations. Toshali, Tamralipi, and Samapa – their names resonated like distant echoes, each holding a fragment of Kalinga's tumultuous history. From *Vidushaka* to *Bitathya*, these agents of Magadha had seamlessly integrated themselves into the fabric of Kalinga Society, their senses tuned to every whisper of dissent or resistance.

Sarpa, the wizened Chief of Intelligence, expounded upon the ethical code of espionage devised by Vishnugupta. Merchant spies within fortress walls, ascetic disguised as wanders, and humble farmers positioned on the fringes were part of a vast network designed to gather vital intelligence. Elusive yet essential truths emerged from the very convergence of diverse sources, their veracity confirmed through meticulous cross-referencing.

Amidst the labyrinthine narratives of spies and secrets, Karuvaki grappled with a profound dilemma. Loyalty to her husband, the sovereign of Magadha, clashed with an unwavering allegiance to her native Kalinga. Her heart bled for the atrocities inflicted upon her kith and her kin, yet she harboured no illusions about the complexities of geopolitics and power.

As the tales unfolded, painting vivid portraits of wartime manoeuvres and post-war tribulations, Karuvaki's resolve crystallized. She would become the harbinger of reconciliation, a beacon of hope amidst the shadows of conflict. She would unearth the truths buried beneath layers of deception and sorrow for her beloved Emperor, trapped in remorse.

With every revelation from the spies, Karuvaki's determination surged. She was resolved to bridge the chasm between conqueror and conquered, weaving an amalgam of empathy and understanding in a realm fraught with division. The scars of war would not define her husband's legacy; redemption would be their shared triumph.

In the corridors of power, amidst the echoes of distant battles, Karuvaki stood resolute. Her quest for redemption had only just begun, a testimony to a Queen's the enduring strength, love and the indomitable spirit of a queen determined to heal a fractured empire.

The story of the day ended here after a long tale of confusion and truth elicitation. The rock elephant looked calmly at the two calm and confused faces.

"Clarity is going to precipitate over the churned curd; the butter is going to clean out!" said the rock elephant.

Budu and Kalu saluted the rock elephant and turned towards their village.

[Piyadasi]

Avijita Kalinga

Early in the afternoon, Kalu and Budu, two eager individuals, walked to the hill and the rock elephant. They carried an offering of ladu, ready to worship the divine soul. As they approached, they could hear the murmur of the elephant, a sound that filled them with anticipation.

The rock elephant, a majestic creature with weathered features and a wise gaze, spoke. "I am glad that I have two patient listeners. The stories that were coiled in my memory are being ventilated, and I feel free," it murmured.

"It is all your grace and our good luck that we hear from you," Kalu and Budu uttered simultaneously.

The voice of the rock elephant came to the story part and continued.

"A brief account of the then Kalinga was presented by the Chief of Intelligence, with his team, the Magadha Intelligence Panel, many of them carrying on the sequence of description ahead. They rendered their opinions as follows –

"Kalinga, then situated in the eastern reaches of Jambudvipa (ancient India), was a kingdom steeped in antiquity, tracing its origins back to the times immortalized in Ramayana and Mahabharata. These narratives depict Kalinga as a sovereign political entity with distinct geographic boundaries and unique cultural attributes. It was never conquered before by any power. This is a testament to its resilience and the awe-inspiring cultural heritage it holds. This heritage was unmatched by any other kingdom in Jambudvipa, even Magadha, who spread its paws to east and west, north and south, somehow skipping Kalinga up to the time of the third Emperor, Piyadasi Raja."

Geographically, Kalinga was a sight to behold. With its rushing stream and cool breeze, the majestic Ganges River served as a formidable boundary to the north. To the south, the Godavari River's gentle flow and soothing sounds, marked another significant edge. The eastern frontiers of Kalinga were embraced by the vast Kalinga Sea, a body of water that played a crucial role in shaping the maritime identity and prowess of the kingdom. Inland, Kalinga was adorned with undulating mountain ranges, their peaks reaching for the sky, and lush forests, their leaves rustling in the wind, teeming with diverse flora and fauna, creating a picturesque and impervious backdrop against potential invaders, a description that fills the readers with awe and admiration.

Kalinga's maritime heritage was legendary, dating back to ancient times referenced in the Ramayana. The kingdom's sailors and navigators were celebrated for their seafaring prowess, venturing far across the Kalinga Sea to distant lands, including the fabled Golden Islands (*Suvarnadvipa*). These islands, rich in gold and spices like cloves, were a testament to Kalinga's extensive trade networks and maritime dominance. This dominance, coupled with their formidable military prowess, is a fascinating aspect of Kalinga's history that intrigues historians and enthusiasts alike.

Kalinga's significance transcended mere boundaries; it was a realm steeped in myth, history, and culture. The forested lands of *Panchavati,* traversed by Rama, Laxmana and Sita during their exile in *Treta Yuga*, epitomized the enduring connection between Kalinga and epic lore. The abduction of Sita by the demon king Ravana, who transported her across the sea to Sri Lanka in the celestial vehicle *Puspaka Vimana*, further underscored Kalinga's prominence in ancient narratives. Valmiki Muni had made a lot of effort in his epic to trace the abducted Sita through the Kalingan sailors if at all she had been carried away somewhere in the sea.

The kingdom's cultural and economic vibrancy and strategic geographic location made Kalinga a pivotal regional power and influence point. Piyadasi Ashoka, the illustrious Maurya Emperor known for his profound wisdom and military prowess, acknowledged Kalinga's historical significance.

The recounting of Kalinga's glorious history weaves together elements of myth, legend, and historical context, showcasing the kingdom's enduring legacy as a bastion of maritime trade, cultural exchange, and ancient wisdom within the tapestry of Indian Civilization.

During the Mahabharata era, Kalinga was not a singular entity but a collection of powerful kingdoms, each contributing to the rich fabric of ancient India. Its alliances and engagements with prominent figures and events from the epic Mahabharata underscored the kingdom's historical significance.

One notable aspect highlighted in the Mahabharata war Kalinga's alliance with the *Kauravas*, particularly Duryodhana, the eldest of *Kaurava* princes. A Kalinga princess wedded to Duryodhana exemplified the kingdom's strategic importance and diplomatic ties within the broader political landscape of ancient India.

The king of Kalinga, identified as a trusted advisor of

the *Kauravas*, played a pivotal role during the Mahabharata War. His counsel and leadership were instrumental in marshalling the formidable Kalinga forces comprising infantry, elephantry (war elephants), and cavalry to bolster the Kaurava ranks against their adversaries, the *Pandavas* and their allies.

The Kalinga contingent deployed to the battlefield represented a formidable military presence, notably the *Nishad* wing, commanded by the son of King Srutayudha. This regiment, comprised of seasoned warriors from Kalinga's forested tracts, brought a fierce and penetrating force to the conflict, showcasing the kingdom's martial prowess and strategic capabilities. Such capable foot soldiers and archers were innumerable in the Atavi land that comprised the western fold of Kalinga.

The story of the Atavi tribes adjacent to Kalinga's harbour sparkled with martial tradition and archery expertise, reminiscent of the legendary Ekalabya from the Mahabharata. These tribes had long been renowned for their prowess and had played a significant role in Kalinga's military circle for generations.

In the lush forests and hilly terrain surrounding Kalinga, the Atavi tribes have honed their skills as expert archers. From a young age, their life revolved around martial training, mastering the bow and arrow with unparalleled precision. Each member of these tribes possessed remarkable marksmanship, comparable to the skill exhibited by Ekalabya in the ancient epic.

The Atavi tribes were vital to Kalinga's military, contributing their unique talents and fierce dedication to the kingdom's defence. They were recruited into various military wings, including specialized dragoon units known for their agility and effectiveness in battle.

Within Kalinga's military structure, these Atavi warriors were esteemed for their ability to navigate dense forests, scale rugged terrains, and deliver deadly accurate strikes with their bows. Their archery skills were unparalleled, and they had earned a reputation as elite fighters capable of turning the tide of the battle.

As the story unfolds the Atavi's role in Kalinga's military became central to the kingdom's defence and strategic operations. Their connection to the ancient traditions of archery and warfare adds depth and authenticity to Kalinga's martial culture, showcasing their resilience and tenacity in the face of adversity. Their unwavering dedication and unmatched skills command respect and admiration, making them iconic figures within Kalinga's military history.

Through their exploits and contributions, the Atavi tribes emerge as iconic figures within Kalinga's military history, embodying the spirit of courage and skill that defines the kingdom's legacy in warfare.

As the Magadha intelligence panel reported, Karuvaki, a proud native of Kalinga, felt a surge of pride upon learning of her kingdom's historical contributions and military strength. She admired her people's courage and strategic understanding, which prompted her to question why her husband, the Emperor, opted for an aggressive approach rather than pursuing a path of diplomacy and peace.

In delving into the intricacies of Mahabharata lore and the diverse array of undercover agents and intelligence networks operating within the ancient Indian landscape, Karuvaki contemplated the deeper motivations and strategic considerations that might have influenced her husband's decision-making during the turbulent times of the Kalinga War.

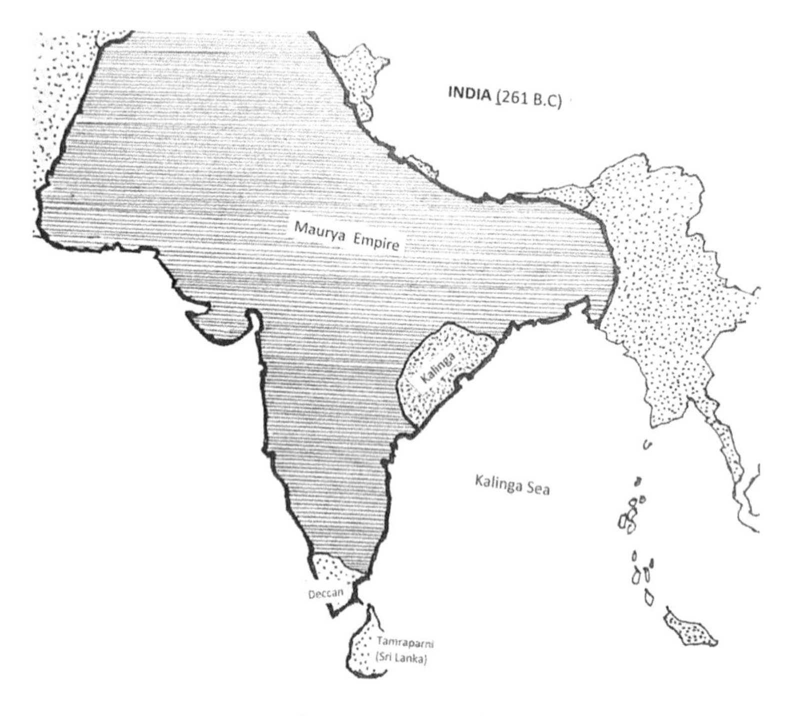

[Avijita Kalinga]

This narrative thread enriches the story's historical backdrop, shedding light on Kalinga's legacy as a critical player in the epic saga of ancient India. It intertwined myth, diplomacy, and military prowess within the grand tapestry of the Mahabharata narrative.

As revealed to the Queen through the intelligence network, Kalinga's religious fervour unveiled a rich tapestry of Jainism deeply interwoven with the kingdom's culture and identity. The white-clothed spy, masquerading as a sage, *sannyasi,* brought forth a wealth of information about Kalinga's spiritual landscape, and mainly centred on the worship of Kalingajina, the crowned deity revered by the people.

Kalinga's devotion to Jainism spanned centuries and

all twenty-four Tirthankaras were held responsible in high esteem by the populace. The first *Tirthankara*, Risabhanatha, embodied in the image of *Kalingajina* with a majestic crown, had revered place as the State Deity of Kalinga with the ideals of *Ahimsa* (non-violence), Truthfulness, *Aparigraha* (non-attachment). Also *Achourya* or Asteya (non-stealing) were deeply ingrained in Kalinga's religious ethos.

This religious fervour intrigued in the Emperor, who sought to understand Kalinga Jina's popularity and influence among the people. The spy revealed that Kalinga Jina was revered by the royal and wealthy classes and adored by the common folk. These people took great pride in Jain culture and considered the deity as iconic figure representing Kalinga's society.

Inquiring further, the Emperor sought clarity on the political landscape of Kalinga, learning about the existence of two significant regions known historically as east and west Kalinga, each with capital Rajapur and Sighapur. Despite these distinctions, the spy revealed that when faced with external threats or cultural events, the Kalingas demonstrated a remarkable unity, akin to a herd of wild buffaloes rallying against a common adversary, as if all their horns combined into one, showcasing their strength and resilience.

The Emperor's interest was piqued by the spy's detailed explanation of the religious cohesion within Kalinga. The Kalingas, he learned, exhibited intense and unwavering inclination towards their faith, surpassing the complexity of *Sanatana Dharma*. Despite the variations in their religious beliefs, they managed to forge a cohesive front, presenting a united and formidable force in matters of defence or cultural pride.

Karuvaki absorbed this detailed information, and

gained insight into Kalinga's deep-rooted religious and cultural foundations. The revelations shed light on the complexities of governance and the unique socio-religious dynamics that shaped the kingdom's identity and resilience over generations. 2

She couldn't trace how such a natural Kalinga could attract her husband's military mindset! She suspected the day he was anointed, a trait of imperialism entered his mind from the weight of the throne. Otherwise, he would have been moving inside his territory, confined to it.

She was looking here and there to ascertain the region of the infiltration and the war.

After much of the story, the rock elephant took a long pause, and both the listeners were sure that the day's talk of the master *raconteur* was over. They looked at the face of the elephant, stood a while and saluted. It was their salute to take leave.

They got down, tracing their way to the country lane with some discussion in a low voice.

The Land of Black War Elephants

As Kalu and Budu reflected on the story of the unconquered native Kalinga, they felt a sense of pride and satisfaction in their ancestors' resilience. It was a natural human tendency to admire the bravery and fortitude of those who came before them, especially at a time when people lived in harmony with nature and followed their paths without the constraints of modern society.

With the dawn of a new day, Kalu and Budu could hardly contain their excitement as they readied themselves to revisit the rock elephant. Their hearts were filled with eager anticipation for the continuation of the tale. Gathering the customary offerings, they made their way to the sacred spot, their steps buoyed by reverence and devotion.

Arriving at the site as the sun began its ascent, they greeted the divine presence with humble prostrations, paying homage to the ancient soul that dwelled within the rocky form. The elephant, ever attentive to their presence, welcomed them with its familiar whispers, signalling the beginning of another chapter in its timeless narrative.

As the story unfolded, the elephant picked up from where it had left off, seamlessly weaving together the threads of history and legend. With each word uttered by the ancient storyteller, Kalu and Budu found themselves drawn deeper into the rich curtains of the past, captivated by the tales of bravery, betrayal, and redemption that unfolded before them.

In that sacred moment, amidst the whispers of the rock elephant and the gentle rustle of the wind, Kalu and Budu felt a profound connection to their ancestors and the land that had shaped their lives. It was a reminder of the enduring power of storytelling to transcend time and space, binding past, present and future in a continuous cycle of remembrance and renewal.

As they listened intently to the words of the rock elephant, Kalu and Budu were reminded of the importance of preserving the wisdom of the past and passing it on to future generations. Those ancient stories lay the keys to understanding who they were, where they came from, and where they were destined to go. And as they departed from the sacred site, their hearts were filled with gratitude for the opportunity to be part of something greater than themselves, a timeless legacy that would endure long after they were gone.

The Queen Consort listened intently as *Dahuka*, the disguised Magadha intelligencer, recounted the intricate details of Kalinga's military and trade relationships. He focused mainly on the prized elephants. The hallmark of Kalinga's martial prowess was the robust wild black tuskers.

It was difficult for a spy to reach everywhere in the dress and words foreign to the natives. *Dahuka,* posing as an *Ayurvedic* herbal researcher treating joint disorders of a Kalinga royal military advisor, gleaned invaluable insights into the unique nature of Kalinga's elephants. These majestic beasts were known for their immense size and strength, distinguished by their darker complexion compared to varieties from Magadha and Anga. Though challenging to train, the skilled Kalinga Mahuntas – elephant catchers and trainers – were adept enough at preparing them for military use, recruiting and conditioning hundreds of young tuskers for warfare.

The advisor shared intriguing historical perspectives, suggesting that the long-standing relationship between Kalinga and neighbouring kingdoms like – Anga, Banga, and Magadha - including gifting or purchasing trained war elephants, has been around since ancient times, dating back to the eras of Jarasandha and Mahabharata, and Nanda Kings just after a kingdom was assigned a definite territory.

This exchange enriched the military capabilities of recipient kingdoms and facilitated royalty's movement and transportation. Needs across Kalinga's terrain itself were challenging and largely unsuitable for chariots. Dahuka expressed keen interest in exposing Kalinga's premier elephantry with the latest innovations and strategies.

Black Elephants of Kalinga

However, his inquiries aroused suspicion, leading the Kalinga military advisor to confront him as a suspected Magadha spy. Fortunately, Dahuka managed to evade capture, likening his escape to slipping away from the clutches of a leopard in the jungle. Undeterred, Dahuka swiftly assumed the guise of a Jain *arhat,* delving deeper into Kalinga's jungles and military encampments to uncover clandestine tactics and manoeuvres unknown to Magadha troops. His relentless pursuit of intelligence underscored the intricate dynamics of espionage and the high stakes in navigating the complex relations between neighbouring kingdoms during this political intrigue and military prowess era.

As Dahuka's escapades unfolded, the Queen Consort marvelled at the extent of Magadha's espionage network and the lengths to which its agents would go to acquire strategic insights crucial for the kingdom's security and diplomatic manoeuvring in the ever-evolving landscape of ancient India.

Dahuka, the seasoned intelligence agent, immersed himself in the awe-inspiring historical evolution of the use of elephants in warfare, delving into the insight of ancient elephant trainers and the annals of pre-Mahabharata days. Through his interactions with these experts, Dahuka gained a profound understanding of how the mastodon – the majestic war elephant trainers – became not only a symbol of military strength but also a crucial determinant of a kingdom's rank and power. In the context of India's imperial ambitions, Magadha epitomized the strategic importance of elephants in warfare under kings like Bimbisara and successive rulers, each striving to outdo the other in expanding the kingdom's dominion and military might. Elephantry, once a simple component of royal entourages for tours and travel, evolved into a sophisticated corps capable of frontline combat with elephant-back archery and spear-throwing.

When Maurya ascended to power in Magadha, they faced maintaining their elephantry. The Chief Minister, Chanakya astutely identified the Kalinga tuskers as black and robust, making them the most suitable for military purposes. This strategic choice elevated the Kalinga tuskers to superiority in the pachyderm force, a testament to the Maurya's military prowess.

Dahuka marvelled at how sovereigns carefully managed the franchise of mastodon power to consolidate and project the power structure of their kingdoms. In particular, the contrast between Magadha and Kalinga was stark. Magadha's Emperors, seated on their thrones, cast their eyes southward towards Kalinga, always mindful of the formidable pachyderms peering with fierce eyes from the rugged hinterlands of this inaccessible kingdom.

Magadha vs. Kalinga

Intelligence gathered hinted at historical interactions between Magadha and Kalinga, with tales of potential elephant acquisitions or strategic alliances. Dahuka wondered about the scale and impact of such dealings, notably when the Maurya records documented an impressive mastodon force of nearly seven thousand war elephants.

Meanwhile, the Queen Consort eagerly awaited the intelligence brought by Dahuka. In her vision, a stable protective shield of elephants symbolizes the mighty defence of her beloved motherland. Her familial allegiances and geopolitical considerations, though significant, paled in comparison to her primary focus, which was alleviating her husband's mental anguish. This relentless pursuit of resolution, akin to a drowning person grasping at a straw was the strength of her love.

As Dahuka's narrative unfolded, intertwining the threads of history, politics, and military strategy, the Queen balanced personal emotions with statecraft's necessities. Her thoughts oscillated like a pendulum between competing loyalties and pressing concerns for her husband's well-being and the realm.

A story is set at this step; the rock elephant breathed a sigh. A rock elephant in Kalinga is a mock to the natural mastodon folk. How could Piyadasi Raja think of installing a rock mimic in the land of elephants?

Gautama Saugata's birth story must have mused the Raja. A white elephant was the omen for his dream-expectant mother, Maya Devi. The rock elephant revealed, 'He vested in me the heavenly potency as a remorseful restitutory gift to Kalinga from his heavy heart. That is my stand here, though people your age are unaware."

The whisper fainted daily tailing off to the end of the day's story.

Both guys wished for the divine rock elephant and started retreating to their village. They were so impressed that the story reverberated in cyclical rhythm.

The Kalinga Sea and Kalinga Vessel

Kalu and Budu, punctual as always, embarked on their journey to Dhauli Hill with a sense of urgency, knowing they couldn't afford to be late for their meeting with the rock elephant. With each step, their anticipation grew, fuelled by the ancient site's mystery and wonder.

Budu's curiosity about the rock elephant's divine insight grew as they journeyed, a fascination he couldn't shake. How could a mere carved figure possess such profound knowledge of the past and the world? Kalu, however, reminded him of the rock elephant's divine origins, a creation of artisans under the Emperor's command. The presence of the Airabat, the celestial elephant, was undeniable, infusing the rock with a sacred energy that transcended mortal understanding.

Budu's curiosity only deepened as they approached the hill, prompting him to inquire about the origin of his name. Why was it called Dhauli Hill? It was a question that had long lingered in his mind, and he was eager to uncover the truth finally.

Upon their arrival, after offering their customary prayers and ladu to the divine elephant, Budu summoned the courage to voice his question. With bated breath, he awaited the rock elephant's response, hoping for clarity on the matter that had intrigued him for so long.

In its ancient and breathy voice, the rock elephant began to weave a tale of the hill's past. It spoke of a time when the mountain lay barren and desolate, shunned by the people who feared its association with the death and decay. But everything changed with the arrival of a team from Takshashila, sent by the Emperor Piyadasi to carve out the form of the rock elephant.

Under the Emperor's command, the artisans meticulously crafted the divine figure, imbuing it with sacred significance. And as the hill transformed, so too did its name. Known simply as the 'White Hill' in the local tongue, it took on the moniker of Dhauli, signifying its newfound purity and sanctity. This renaming was a significant event in the history of the hill, marking its transformation from a barren and desolate place to a sacred site of worship and pilgrimage.

The word 'Dhauli' or white is from my name, Seto or Sweto, i.e. white from the Buddhist concept of the Divine White Elephant, *Airabata,* the mother of Gautam dreamed of during the period of her conception. White name here is pious; it bears its association with divine nomenclature.

For Kalu and Budu, the revelation brought a sense of satisfaction and fulfilment. They had sought answers, and now they had them, woven into the fabric of the hill's history by the ancient wisdom of the rock elephant. As they departed from the sacred site, their hearts were filled with gratitude for the opportunity to uncover the past mysteries and to commune with the divine presence that dwelled within.

After a moment's gap, the elephant started the story of the day on the Kalinga maritime matter, as the intelligence team, led by *Sarpa Mahamatra,* explained to Queen Karuvaki. The basics were already known to the Queen as a resident of the region.

Karuvaki, a wise baby of a Kalinga ruler, eagerly absorbed the insights gleaned from the multifaceted spies who unravelled the secrets of 'Avijita Kalinga, the unconquered realm renowned for its formidable military might and the natural prowess embodied by the mighty war elephants. As she turned her attention towards *Sarpa Mahamatra,* the intelligence chief, she anticipated further revelations from Magadha's professional assets. The Queen's role was to oversee the kingdom's affairs and make strategic decisions on the Emperor's mental depression based on the informations provided by her advisors and intelligence team.

Sarpa Mahamatra, aware of the strategic significance of maritime affairs in the region, broached a critical issue that had hitherto remained unexplored – the domain where Magadha's vested interests intersected with Kalinga's naval power. Here, a telling incident from seven years earlier, when the newly anointed Emperor expressed his dissatisfaction with the marine and navel administration of the realm, was counted. *Sarpa Mahamatra*'s role was to gather and analyze intelligence, and provide strategic advice to the Queen for the sake of relieving the gloomy Emperor.

During a routine administrative review, the Emperor, a visionary leader well-versed in Chanakya's *Arthashastra,* which emphasized the importance of maritime trade, rebuked the maritime officials, questioning their competence and ambition. "Are you content to swim in the Ganges, or will you sail the eastern seas like traders in *Ratnakar,* the sea to the west of India, some call it the Arabian Sea," was his orders. This led to a shift in the kingdom's maritime strategy.

The *Amatya* of Maritime Affairs, a key figure in

Magadha's administration, was taken aback by the Emperor's admonishment. He dared not to disclose the reality – that much of India's coastal trade was dominated independently by Kalinga, with Magadha forced to navigate the tributaries and pay dues for any exports or imports through Kalinga's Tamluk port. His role was to manage and oversee all the maritime affairs of the kingdom, including trade and naval administration.

Sensing the underlying challenge, the wise Emperor hinted at a future strategy shift, "Time will tell it we can establish meaningful maritime trade along the Eastern coast," was her suggestion. As a result, a cohort of undercover operatives was swiftly dispatched to infiltrate Kalinga's bustling ports and coastal towns. Disguised as magicians (*Shouvikas*), grocery shopkeepers, petty *Ayurvedic* practitioners (*Dhanantwari*), tailors (*Suchikas*), beggars or small-scale mechanics, these agents assimilated into the fabric of Kalinga maritime communities. They aim to glean intelligence on the intricacies of marine execution, trade routes, and commercial secrets.

Over the ensuing months, the covert operatives meticulously documented titbits of maritime operations, enriching Magadha's intelligence database with invaluable insights into Kalinga's maritime activities. From bustling ports like Tamluk to coastal hubs such as Dantapura, Palura, Samapa, and Pithunda, these spies surreptitiously observed and reported on the movement of ships, the flow of goods and the nuances of trade networks.

As the Queen absorbed these revelations, she grasped the geopolitical ramifications underlying Magadha's interest in the Kalinga maritime domain. The intelligence gathered by Sarpa Mahamatra's network of operatives opened a new frontier in understanding the complex dynamics of marine trade power and its implications for the strategic interests of Magadha and Kalinga. In her quest to unravel the mysteries that plagued her husband's troubled reign, the Queen recognized the pivotal role of maritime intelligence in shaping the course of history, a disclosure that filed her with anticipation for what was to come.

Aveda, the Magadha spy supervisor, arrived at Tamluk (Tamralipi Port) with a specific mission: to oversee the progress of the espionage operations aimed at unsnarling the maritime and trade affairs of this vital domain within the dreamland of Magadha's imperial ambitions. Compared to seasoned sailors or shipbuilders, Aveda needed more experience in vessel construction or the nuance of the sea voyages to distant isles. His intelligence-gathering and extraction expertise demanded astute observation and meticulous documentation.

Tasked by *Sarpa Mahamatra*, Aveda was accompanied by a group of operatives including *Hatakar* – a proficient forceful entry expert disguised as a local emissary – and several dozen wanderer *Gudhapusushas* (undercover agents) who scoured the bustling port like ants drawn to molasses. Their mission was clear: infiltrating, observing, and extracting critical intelligence on Tamluk's maritime activities.

Yet, penetrating the intricate web of Tamluk's bustling port proved a Herculean task. The port, a mainstay of India's passenger and cargo trade, operated relentlessly, exhibiting little regard for individual personalities or kingdoms. This indifference was a thorn in an expanding empire that thrived on hegemonic diplomacy and persuasive rhetoric.

Aveda's operatives faced numerous challenges. The language barrier posed a significant hurdle, with foreigners arriving from distant islands speaking an utterly incomprehensible dialect to the Magadha spies. Moreover, the Magadhi accent and demeanour elicited distrust among the port natives and daily wage workers, who viewed Magadha's imperial presence with suspicion and disdain.

Boita to and fro

The gudhapurushas, needing more fluency in the international port's language, relied on guesswork and gestures to navigate this unfamiliar terrain. The arrival of visitors from the Suvarnadvipa, or 'golden islands', further complicated the situation, as their customs and gestures remained mysterious to the undercover operatives.

Queen Karuvaki's restlessness and curiosity reached a crescendo amid this intricate web of espionage. "What is happening? Could this be a ploy to goad my husband into waging war on pretences?" she questioned, her concern clearly perceptible.

Aveda, taken aback by the Queen's directness, gathered his composure and began to recount the convoluted diplomatic plot that had unfolded under his watchful eye. With the permission of Sarpa Mahamatra, he detailed the intricate workings of a scheme rooted in economic strategy. Magadha had long grappled with challenges in importing gold from Siberia and China via the Silk Route beyond the Himalayas. The Suvarna Dvipa islands, a popular name among Kalinga sailors, served as a crucial intermediary hub, with Sumatra emerging as a critical node in the complex trade web.

Under Magadha's banner, special cargo ships imported gold to Tamluk, a strategic port, where it was stored in Magadha's yard. While piracy in the Kalinga Sea was rare, occasional incidences along the western shore of Ratnakar posed a different challenge.

The narrative unravelled further as Aveda explained the strategic intent behind charging Tamluk with piracy by Kalinga pirates – a move aimed at extracting revenue or punitive measures from the port. However, the overarching objective was not to disrupt the ordinary relations between Magadha and Kalinga but to assert Magadha's authority through taxation and regulation.

Enlightened by these revelations, Queen Karuvaki pieced together the narrative threat that had fuelled her husband's imperialistic fervour – a flame that had burned bright across dynasties past. As she grappled with the implications of this intricate geopolitical dance, the Queen's understanding deepened, revealing the complex interplay of power, ambition, and diplomacy in the ancient kingdoms of Magadha and Kalinga.

In the west end of Kaushambi, two wise emissaries chosen by *Sarpa,* the Head of Intelligence, sat in silence, awaiting the moment to share their insights with Queen Karuvaki. Their mission was crucial: to gather accurate assessments of the coastline near Toshali, the capital of Kalinga. These coastlines, characterized by rugged cliffs and hidden coves, were a strategic gateway to the kingdom, and understanding their intricacies was part of a broader effort to aid the Emperor's recovery by disclosing the mysteries that plagued his mind.

The *Sarpa Mahamatra,* fully aware of the situation's urgency, hinted to the emissaries to respond to the Queen's inquiries. He understood that their evidence was not just vital but crucial to curing the Emperor's derangement. In this current state, the Emperor needed help to make sound decisions or govern effectively. The need for accurate assessments of the coastlines near Toshali was not just essential, but urgent.

Kalinga Boita

The first emissary, stationed to spy on Samapa – an inland river port north of the Kalinga Sea on the eastern bank of the Rushikulya River – provides a vivid account of Kalinga's bustling trade and commerce. At Samapa's inland port, a diverse array of goods, including food staples like rice and maize, luxury items like silk and spices, and unique crafts made from local materials like stone wood, were loaded onto cargo ships bound for distant destinations like Tamraparni (Sri Lanka), Java, Sumatra and Bali and days passed with continuous loading, underscoring the vibrant maritime activity that defined Kalinga's economic lifeblood.

However, the journey began at something other than Samapa. Instead, it started at Palura, a place of great significance. Situated at the confluence of the Rushikulya River and the Kalinga Sea, Palura's strategic location and well-developed port facilities made it a crucial departure point for Kalinga's maritime trade. Here the kingdom forged its connections to distant lands and sustained its economic prosperity.

The Samapa Emissary could inform the naval chief of detailed stories of great financial background, who immediately conveyed them to the Emperor. It contained crucial facts about gem-rich Atavi Land and diamond business through Palura port to the international market.

The *Gudhapurusha's* revelation about the gem trade of Kalinga and its ties to the Chief of Atavi Land and merchants sent shockwaves through the royal court, stirring a pot of intrigue. Queen Karuvaki, her curiosity piqued, was drawn into the unfolding drama as the full implications of this trade arrangement were unveiled.

It became apparent that the Atavi Land, particularly the influential estate of Asuragarh, held strategic importance for Kalinga's economy and defence. Asuragarh was a seat o f valuable gemstones and a vital hub for maritime trade, facilitating the export of these precious gems to distant markets.

The Emperor's response to this news was a mix of worry and anger, his heart heavy with the burden of

Kalinga's exploitation. First, he considered the gems and diamonds from Asuragarh to be assets of the Maurya Emperor. Without rhyme or reason, he claimed the gem-rich Atavi hinterland of Kalinga as Maurya's. Secondly, he lamented the outsiders' plundering of Kalinga's natural resources, seeing it as a severe failure by the Kalinga administration. The Emperor was resolute that the wealth from local mines should stay inside the country rather than be exported and the assets solely belonged to the Mauryas.

Within the corridors of power, discussions ensued on diplomatically addressing this issue. The Emperor contemplated the need for stricter vigilance and regulation of Kalinga's gem trade, ensuring that the lucrative industry's economic benefits flowed back to his empire's treasury.

Meanwhile, gem merchants continued their business in the vibrant markets of Asuragarh and other Atavi estates, blissfully unaware of the mounting concerns within the imperial court. Kalinga's gemstones, renowned for their quality and scarcity, found eager buyers from far-flung lands, enriching the merchants and bolstering the kingdom's reputation as a hub of exquisite gemcraft.

Queen Karuvaki, a beacon of wisdom, pondered the delicate balance between economic prosperity and sovereignty. She recognized the importance of maintaining Kalinga's economic autonomy while judging the ownership of the gem-filled Atavi Lands of Kalinga now claimed by the Emperor. As discussions unfolded within the court, the Queen, with her keen intellect, sought to ensure that any measure taken would uphold the integrity and prosperity of Kalinga while addressing the Emperor's concerns about external influence and exploitation of local resources.

Meanwhile, the second *Gudhapurusha,* stationed at Palura, was bewildered by the relentless marine traffic – a testament to the ceaseless arrivals and departures of cargo ships plying routes between Palura and *Suvarnadvipa*, Tamraparni, Brahmadesh, and various Far East isles inhabited by Kalingans. With its constant flow of goods and people, this bustling maritime trade indicated Kalinga's economic strength and ability to connect with the broader world.

The tale of Dantapura, Kalinga's capital harbour, was captivating. The harbour was home to a Buddhist Stupa, a testament to the faith and courage of Guhasiva. He believed a Buddha relic housed within the stupa protected him from invaders. To safeguard this relic, Guhasiva entrusted the divine tooth to be hidden within his daughter's thick hair – to be safely transported aboard a ship bound for Tamraparni. However, the princess, accompanied by her husband, Dantakumara, set sail from Tamluk port instead, opting for a direct route to Tamraparni.

As the emissaries unravelled the tale of intrigue and trade, Queen Karuvaki's interest was piqued. The intricate web of Kalinga's maritime activity, woven with stories of divine relics and strategic voyages, painted a vibrant picture of a kingdom brimming with life, commerce, and hidden mysteries. Each revelation hinted at the complex tapestry of Kalinga's maritime prowess and rich cultural heritage, offering the Queen a deeper understanding of the kingdom at the heart of her husband's imperial ambitions.

The hall resonated with the whispers of ancient tales, setting the stage for a deeper exploration of Kalinga's enigmatic past and present, exposed by the astute spies of Magadha. These spies, with their keen observations and meticulous documentation, had been instrumental in uncovering Kalinga's hidden truths, providing a reliable source of information for the Queen's understanding of the recent happenings of her motherland.

Sarpa Mahamatra, the intelligence chief of Magadha, concluded his presentation by shedding light on the monumental strategic significance of the Kalinga Sea and its implications for any potential conflict. The sea, frequented by skilled Kalinga sailors and constituting a substantial portion of the kingdom's population, presented a formidable barrier to Magadha's ambitions.

From the perspective of Magadha's intelligence apparatus, the prospect of engaging in conflict with Kalinga at that juncture was a strategic dilemma. The genuine concern was the fear of Kalinga's vast wealth and resources spiralling away to overseas colonies in the eastern seas before Magadha could secure its hold. Kalinga's extensive fleet of vessels, ranging from large *Uru* or *Boita* ships designed for long-distance voyages to smaller *Patmar* vessels equipped with sails, posed a logistical nightmare for Magadha. The sheer number of boats in Kalinga's ports, capable of swiftly evacuating men and treasures, rendered any attempt to subdue Kalinga through conventional means highly challenging.

In practical terms, the Mauryan forces could muster approximately six soldiers for every soldier of Kalinga, and even Magadha's army would equal the whole Kalinga population, illustrating the vast numerical advantage of Magadha. However, the potential for Kalingans to escape or resist through the sea, leveraging their maritime prowess akin to agile fish slipping through nets, added a layer of complexity to Magadha's strategic calculus.

The Emperor found himself in a quandary, torn between the allure of Kalinga's wealth and the logistical nightmare posed by its maritime capabilities. He perceived

Kalinga's non-compliance with tax demands as an act of defiance from a prosperous state. Handling this situation required careful consideration and strategic planning from every level of the Magadha administration.

For Queen Karuvaki, *Sarpa Mahamatra*'s analysis was a revelation. It illuminated the stark realities and challenges inherent in her husband's imperial ambitions *vis-a-vis* Kalinga. The intricacies of naval power, wealth preservation, and strategic mobility underscored the dynamic nature of geopolitical strategy in then-India, shaping the fate of kingdoms and empires alike. As she absorbed these insights, her mind began to churn with the complexities of statecraft and the delicate balance between ambition and pragmatism in pursuit of imperial glory.

As the tall reverberated with the weight of these revelations, the Queen's mind turned to the complexities of statecraft and the delicate balance between ambition and pragmatism in the pursuit of imperial glory.

It was a long day of storytelling. Both the listeners were satisfied and started for their village. They could not think Queen Karuvaki's mind. She must be in a position like Scylla and Charybdis, the destroyed Kalinga and the mentally deranged Emperor. She could not think of the motherland, which was her fascination but was history. Instead, her husband's amelioration was desired instantaneously.

She prayed to the Almighty to give her enough strength and mental judgement to tide over the issue and get her husband recovered.

The Jus and Bellum of Kalinga War

As Kalu, a seasoned tourist guide and Budu, a young paramedic, made their way to Dhauli Hill, their minds were filled with anticipation for the revelations that awaited them. They had been intrigued by the snippets of history and wisdom imparted by the rock elephant and today promised to be no different. However, Budu couldn't shake a sense of unease as he pondered the potential causes behind the Kalinga War.

His suspicions led him to probe Kalu about any incident involving Kalinga seamen that could have sparked such a drastic response from the Magadha Empire. Kalu confessed that he hadn't heard of any specific incidents, but the possibility of false accusations or provocations couldn't be dismissed outright. With this lingering question in their minds, they hastened their steps, eager to uncover the day's story from the rock elephant.

Upon arrival, they noticed a heightened sense of alert emanating from the rock elephant, a subtle shift from its usual demeanour. Sensing the gravity of the upcoming narrative, they prepared themselves for what lay ahead.

Kalu, acknowledging the solemnity of the moment, greeted the rock elephant respectfully before inquiring about its apparent alertness. With a sombre tone, the rock elephant revealed the weighty nature of the story it was about to convey. It hinted at a truth that would cast its mentor and creator, Emperor Piyadasi, in a less-than-flattering light. Despite this, the elephant assured of us the grievances caused by his actions.

As the listeners braced for the unfolding tale, they understood they were about to witness a narrative fraught with complexity and moral ambiguity. They listened intently, knowing that the truths revealed by the rock elephant would challenge their perceptions and provoke reflection on the nature of justice, war, and the responsibilities of those in power. The Kalinga War, they knew, was not a simple tale of conquest but a complex web of political intrigue, moral dilemma and the human cost of power.

The rock elephant's citation of Emperor Piyadasi's warning to the Atavi people as mentioned in the earliest rock edict in Aramaic scripts today labelled as the Thirteenth Rock Edict is a profound contemplation among Kalu and Budu. The inclusion of such a warning amidst Ashoka's expressions of remorse for the suffering inflicted upon the people of Kalinga hinted at a more profound complexity surrounding the region's post-war dynamics.

Historically, Kalinga's military strength was often intertwined with its aboriginal and tribal populations, who had formed formidable forces such as the *Nishat* wing led by figures like Bhanumat centuries before Ashoka's reign. Even centuries later, during the rule of Mahameghavahana Kharavela, the tribal tracts, known as the eighteen Vidyadhara states, remained pivotal to Kalinga's military prowess. These regions were renowned for their skilled archers and elephant trainers, further augmenting Kalinga's military might.

The warning issued to the Atavi people a year after the

Kalinga War suggested a lingering concern about potential rebellion or resistance in the region. It implied that Ashoka was not just dealing with a straightforward conquest but potentially faced challenges from guerrilla warfare tactics employed by the Atavi people in their mountainous territories. The Atavi people's resilience, they knew, was a significant factor in the post-war dynamics, and their resistance posed a severe challenge to Magadha's control.

The Atavi tract, encompassing the Mahakantara region of Kalinga and extending into the KBK districts with Bastar in the west, held strategic significance. It was known for its abundance of gemstones, particularly in Indravana (modern Kalahandi district), and the Maurya Empire had its greed for valuable gemstones. Magadha attempted to overcome the sovereignty of Kalinga and prohibit its gemstone trade from vassal Atavi Indravana territory. But Kalinga maintained its independence and continued its market dealings with the Atavi diamonds and gemstones.

The prohibition orders issued by the Magadha administration to Asuragarh, a key stronghold in the Atavi land, reflected the tension between the two powers. Despite not being a vassal or subordinate kingdom, Asuragarh's defiance of Magadha's directives showcased the complexity of the political landscape in the aftermath of the Kalinga War. The Atavi people, known for their resilience and guerrilla warfare tactics, were a significant force in the region, and their resistance to Magadha's control was a testament to their strength and determination.

The narrative hinted at a covert intelligence mission undertaken by Magadha to monitor and control the diamond and gemstone trade in the Mahakantara Atavi land. They understood that the mission was not just a single act of espionage, but a calculated move by Magadha to assert into dominance and control over the region's valuable resources. It underscored the region's strategic importance and the length to which the Magadha Empire was willing to go to maintain its power.

As Kalu and Budu absorbed the intricacies of this historical account, they realized the depth of political manoeuvring and power struggles that characterized the post-war period. The story painted a vivid picture of the complexities that must have been faced before the conflict, offering a deeper understanding of the socio-political dynamics of ancient India.

Coming to the point of what happened just before the conflict, the Samapa emissary, a wise and well-informed diplomat, could inform the naval chief, a trusted advisor to the Emperor, of some detailed stories of stout financial background, who conveyed them to the Emperor immediately. It contained some essential facts about the gem-rich Atavi-Land and the gem business through Palura port to international trade. The emissary and the naval chief of Magadha, they knew, were key players in the unfolding drama, their actions and decisions shaping the course of events.

The Gudhapurusha's revelation about the gem trade of Kalinga and its ties to the Atavi Land's Chief and the merchants sent shockwaves through the royal court, stirring a pot of intrigue. Queen Karuvaki, a woman of intelligence and influence, her curiosity piqued, was drawn into the unfolding drama as the full implications of this trade arrangement were unveiled. Her role, they knew, would be crucial in the events that were about to unfold for reasons to poke into and get a cure for the withdrawn Emperor after months of the war.

It became apparent that the Atavi land, particularly the

influential estate of Asuragarh, held strategic importance for Kalinga's economy and defence. Asuragarh was a seat of valuable gemstones and a vital hub for maritime trade, facilitating the export of these precious gems to distant markets. The gem trade was not just a source of wealth for Kalinga, but also a symbol of its economic independence and prosperity. The gemstone bulk was the most glittering material among the entire export commodities.

Asuragarh was aware of the Cold War situation between Magadha and Kalinga for the last decade, and the last issue was due to the gemstone that the Maurya Empire claimed in vain. Its infantry and archery were prepared to face Magadha at any point of attack.

In the coming days, decisions would be taken safeguarding the Kalinga gem trade and ensure that the kingdom's maritime income must remain a source of price and benefit for its citizens. The intricate web of trade, diplomacy, and governance would shape the future of Kalinga's economy and its relationship with the outside world.

The Emperor's response to this news was full of rage and anger, his heart heavy with the burden of Kalinga's valuable gem trade. He could not conceive that the gemstone mines and valuable stone-carrying riverbeds were in Kalinga's domain. His greed was for the Maurya treasury and he wanted to acquire it at any cost.

Within the corridors of power, discussions ensued on diplomatically addressing this issue. The Emperor contemplated the need for stricter oversight and regulation of Kalinga's gem trade, ensuring that the economic benefits of this lucrative industry flowed back to the Maurya treasury.

Meanwhile, gem merchants carried on with their

business in the vibrant markets of Asuragarh with Kalinga traders and other Atavi Estates, blissfully unaware of the mounting concerns within the imperial court. Kalinga's gemstones, renowned for their quality and scarcity, found eager buyers from far-flung lands, enriching the merchants and bolstering the kingdom's reputation as a hub of exquisite gem craft.

She could recognize the importance of maintaining Kalinga's economic autonomy and the Emperor's concerns about non-realization into the Magadha treasury. The Queen Resort could feel in her interior heart that the valuable gemstone trade was an internal affair of Kalinga, and Magadha had no way to poke her nose except a proposal for purchase, which Magadha never did.

This was the end of the day's story; both the listeners were saddened at the end as they found the insatiable desire of the Magadha Emperor and his imperialistic appetite. Atavi Land, adjacent and within the Kalinga territory was psychologically occupied by the Emperor's thoughts. Rightly, he knew the limits of his empire and Kalinga, but his greed for land and gemstones wrought everything unjustly and infiltrating.

This was the end of today's story; both the listeners were disheartened at the end as they found the insatiable desire of the Magadha Emperor.

Converging upon War

Kalu and Budu arrive on time at the hill and the rock elephant, like they do every other day. They are quick enough today to travel the distance from home in only thirty minutes. They are apprehensive about the story's turn towards a fierce war they had heard.

The rock elephant was also in quite a serious mood. After formal worship with Ladus, the elephant started his tale.

The divergence of ideas and the Emperor's transformation from a grateful son-in-law to a fierce adversary poised for war against Kalinga weighed heavily on Queen Karuvaki's heart and mind. Her deep reflections on the past ten years since her marriage were an intellectual exercise and a journey of emotional turmoil as she sought to unravel the mysteries behind her husband's evolving mindset and imperial ambitions.

In sorrowful circumstances, Piyadasi was thrown out of the palace, and a quarrel among the brothers took such a turn that Father Bindusara did not want him to stay within the limits ofthe Maurya Empire. The only kingdom close to Magadha where he could find shelter was in the south direction, the Kalinga kingdom. This was sometime when Piyadasi put down the rebellion in Ujjain, the capital town of the province of Avantiratha, at age twenty five.

The Queen's recollections took her back to when the

Emperor, then a prince, sought refuge in Kalinga. It was a challenging period of his exile from Magadha when his Father, Bindusara, passed complex orders not to remit him royal assistance. Yet, it was also a time when she witnessed the Magadha Prince's deep gratitude towards Kalinga and its industrious people enriched by their work culture. They had ventured into foreign colonies, expanding their influence beyond the kingdom's borders, a state of prosperity that filled him with admiration.

However, as time passed and the Emperor ascended to the throne, Karuvaki observed a notable shift in his demeanour and ambitions. Initially, a sense of appreciation and indebtedness towards Kalinga had transformed into a monstrous desire for expansion and domination. The seeds of imperial ambition had taken root within him, the growing shoots propelling him towards conquest and conflict.

The Queen pondered the factors that could have influenced this dramatic transformation. Was it the allure of power and conquest inherent in the responsibilities of kingship? Or had external advisors and ministers, eager to expand the kingdom's influence, stocked the flames of ambition, advocating for aggressive policies and expansionist agendas?

Despite the deep connection she shared with the Emperor and their son, Tibal, Karuvaki grappled with the distance that had grown between them. The stresses of governance, the influences of court advisors, and the attraction of imperial glory had reshaped her husband's perspective and priorities. Yet, she remained steadfast in her love and concern for him, demonstrating her strength and resilience.

As Queen Consort, Karuvaki was persistent in understanding the underlying motivations driving her husband's decisions. She harboured no illusions about the complexities of statecraft and diplomacy, recognizing that empires' fate rested on the interplay of personal ambitions, political calculations, and strategic imperatives. The unwavering determination was evidence of her strength and a beacon of inspiration.

In her quest for answers, the Queen resolved to navigate the intricate web of court intrigue and geopolitical dynamics. Her primary concern, above all, remained the well-being of her husband. She hoped to alleviate his mental agony and guide him to a path of wisdom and compassion, which she considered her prime responsibility.

Queen Karuvaki seized with the timeless complexities of power, ambition, and the human spirit in the context of ancient kingdoms and empires as she dived deeper into the enigma of her husband's transformation.

Amidst the tumultuous events in Kalinga and the revelations about Emperor Piyadasi's changing attitudes towards Jainism, Queen Karuvaki had to deal with the profound implications of religious persecution and its impact on her husband's reign.

The Queen's distress deepened as she learned of the extensive spread of Jainism in Kalinga, a land that had embraced the teachings of the Twenty-Fourth *Tirthankara* centuries ago. This revelation struck a chord within her, reflecting Kalinga's cultural richness and spiritual heritage, which initially elicited her husband's admiration.

Emperor Piyadasi's sentiments towards Jains underwent a troubling transformation upon ascending the Magadha throne. He was a man who, in his youth, had been captivated by the cultural richness and spiritual heritage of Kalinga. This land had embraced the teachings of the last Tirthankara of Jainism centuries ago. Yet, his disdain for certain Jain practices, such as *Salehan* – the practice of a voluntary rigorous fast leading to death – was not evident to him. This change in his belief was not a mere shift but a deep-rooted transformation, a product of familial experiences that had left a bitter imprint on his soul. He was reminded of his grandpa's end-stage life. The grandpa left the kingdom and was an arhat of Jainism. He went to Shravanbelagola, a distant south locations where he ended his life with his spiritual mentor. They followed *Salehan*!

As Queen Karuvaki sought to uncover the motivations behind her husband's evolving beliefs, she confronted a stark reality through the testimony of Sumanta, the coachman who had witnessed the desecration of the Jain temple during the Emperor's return journey from Toshali. The destruction was the motive of the Emperor carried out by Magadha army.

Sumanta's account painted a harrowing picture of religious persecution, revealing the brutality inflicted upon Jain monks and adherents. The Queen's heart sank as she contemplated the expanse of inhumanity that had transpired under her husband's command.

Queen Karuvaki was disillusioned and wrecked with moral anguish because of the harsh reality of her husband's actions. The weight of her husband's decisions bore down on her, compelling her to seek redemption and atonement. Her heart was heavy with the burden of her husband's actions, and she straggled with the moral dilemma of standing by him or speaking out against his atrocities.

With an unwavering commitment to righteousness and compassion, Queen Karuvaki made a resolute decision. She would embark on a journey of introspection and spiritual renewal for herself and her husband. She understood the gravity of the sins committed and the urgent need for reconciliation and healing.

Amidst the labyrinthine corridors of power and the intricate complexities of governance, the Queen stood tall as a beacon of unwavering moral clarity. She deftly navigated the moral ambiguities and ethical dilemmas woven into the ancient kingdom's fabric.

As she grappled with the profound implications of religious persecution and its toll on her husband's psyche, Queen Karuvaki embraced her role as a guardian of compassion and righteousness. Her quest for redemption mirrored the enduring struggle between power and conscience, illuminating the timeless complexities of human nature and the pursuit of enlightenment in the face of moral adversity.

With Prince Piyadasi's mind turning imperialistic, the Piyadasi Raja had to travel a great distance of cruelty and torture. The rock elephant took a few moments of pause and rest, with the whisper thinning into silence.

Magadha Diplomacy against the Kalingadhipati

With tears dropping from its eyes, the rock elephant whispered in a sobbing tone that now Magadha decided to thunder on Kalinga, faulty but a prey to imperialism on some vague plea.

The Queen's inquiry into the dynamics of the Magadha-Kalinga relationship revealed a complex web of diplomatic tensions and historical rivalries underpinning the looming spectre of war between the two kingdoms.

Queen Karuvaki, torn between her birthright and her marriage, found herself at the heart of the escalating discord between Magadha and Kalinga. Her inner turmoil, a mix of loyalty and unease, mirrored the complex dynamics of the two kingdoms.

The Diplomatic Head's narrative traced the origins of Magadha's apprehensions towards Kalinga back to the early days of the Maurya dynasty. He explained how internal dissent and rebellion within the Maurya family, coupled with regional unrest, delayed Emperor Piyadasi's ascension to the throne. Despite these challenges, under intelligence guidance, Magadha's External Affairs Department consistently warned the rulers of Toshali, along with the threat of raids and provocations.

The Queen, startled by the shroud of secrecy that veiled these diplomatic manoeuvres, was determined to pierce through it. Her quest for truth and understanding added a layer of suspense to escalating brinkmanship.

The *Sarpa Mahamatra*, Head of Magadha's Intelligence, shifted uncomfortably under the Queen's penetrating gaze. His unease, a visible tension in the room, was evidence of the gravity of the situation. He sought to allay her concerns by revealing insights gleaned from covert operations conducted by the Foreign Affairs Cell.

Yet, the subsequent administration of Emperor Bindusara *Amitraghata* harboured suspicions about these warnings, leading to the initiation of diplomatic correspondence and dispatch of the *Prativedaka* – royal messengers. The *Sarpa Mahamatra* hinted at the clandestine challenges and perils in navigating the treacherous terrain of Magadha-Kalinga relations, a terrain fraught with danger and uncertainty, heightening a sense of tension and unpredictability.

The Queen, burdened with the weight of this revelation, was immersed in a labyrinth of political intrigue and strategic manoeuvring. The narrative underscored the precarious balance of power and the enduring legacy of ancient rivalries that shaped the destiny of kingdoms.

Queen Karuvaki, on hearing the tension between the two kingdoms, was terrified and prayed to the Almighty such a conflict would be aborted. It was not a matching fight between two sides, each with sizeable strength.

The narratives unfolded with the Gudhapurushas revealing the undercurrents of maritime ambition and economic rivalry between Magadha and Kalinga, both vying for access to lucrative overseas trade routes, particularly those leading to the prosperous Silk Route and the spice-rich Eastern Coast.

Magadha, a landlocked kingdom aspiring to expand

its economic reach, sought to capitalize on Kalinga's long-enjoyed maritime wealth. Intrigued by this revelation, Piyadasi Raja, a greedy expectant of Magadha's financial affairs, anticipated the prospects of cooperation and friendship that could arise from shared maritime endeavours.

However, the informer's account swiftly shifted from hope to tension as he detailed Magadha's unsuccessful forays into Kalinga's overseas markets. Disheartened by their lack of success, Magadha's merchants accused Kalinga of wilful neglect and interference in the prosperity of their trade affairs. Some even resorted to highly disruptive behaviour at Tamluk's shipyards, further aggravating the animosity between the two kingdoms and creating a perceptible sense of tension.

The port manager of Tamluk defended Kalinga's trade practices, explaining that they prioritized customer needs and market demand over forced exports that risked unsold goods. This explanation did little to assuage Magadha's grievances, and the situation escalated when Magadha's administration demanded compensation for their perceived losses.

The Queen, deeply troubled and emotionally torn by mounting conflicts fuelled by economic rivalries, reflected on the challenges facing the delicate balance of Magadha-Kalinga relations. The incidents described by the informer painted a picture of strained interactions and misunderstandings driven by commercial ambitions and the pursuit of wealth, evoking a profound sense of empathy in the audience towards the Queen's predicament.

As the Queen absorbed the complexities of these disputes, she couldn't help but feel unease. The constant friction between Magadha and Kalinga, epitomized by the analogy of the tiger and the kid, underscored the precarious nature of their relationship.

In this web of economic tensions and political manoeuvring, the Queen, deeply troubled by the mounting conflicts fuelled by economic rivalries, pondered the implications for her husband's reign and the future of both kingdoms. The narrative illuminated the intricate dance of diplomacy and commerce that defined the interplay between nations, leaving the Queen to navigate the turbulent waters of interstate relations with a mix of cautions, resolve, and a growing sense of uneasiness.

The *Gudhapurusha*'s revelations about the gold import of Magadha through Kalinga's maritime routes, a tale of intrigue and secrecy, piqued the Queen's interest, offering a tantalizing glimpse into the complex web of trade and diplomacy between the two kingdoms.

The Queen's attention sharpened as the informer continued detailing the clandestine import of valuable gold reserves from distant lands like China and Siberia through Sumatra Island. The strategic partnership between Kalinga and Magadha had an ambition of its crucial trade route through the soma of Kalinga but has not received any cooperation amid simmering tensions.

The Queen, eager for more insights, listened intently as the *Gudhapurusha* described the elaborate security measures accompanying these gold shipments. Kalinga's largest *Uru* ships, heavily guarded by Magadha military personnel, navigated treacherous waters to ensure the safe arrival of precious Magadha cargo at Tamluk port. This collaborative effort underscored the intertwined interests of both kingdoms in leveraging maritime resources for economic gain.

However, the informer's narrative took a sad turn

when he mentioned the distrust and scrutiny faced by Magadha Officials upon receiving the imported gold. The Queen sensed the undercurrent of suspicion and paranoia that often clouded interstate transactions, even amidst candid and cooperative endeavours.

The incident at the Tamluk port, marked by a tense exchange between port officials and Magadha scrutinizers, highlighted diplomatic relations' fragility. The Queen, burdened by the weight of these pre-war events, grappled with the escalating tensions that threatened to disentangle the delicate balance between Magadha and Kalinga.

Reflecting on the complexities of maritime trade and interstate politics, the Queen realized the profound implications of these clandestine transactions. The *Gudhapurusha*'s account was a stark reminder of the precarious nature of diplomatic engagements, where economic interests and security concerns intertwined in a delicate dance of cooperation and suspicion.

As the Queen processed the intricate details of this unfolding narrative, she contemplated the broader implications for her husband's reign and the fate of their kingdom. The revelations illuminated the challenges of navigating interstate relations amidst competing interests and ambitions, leaving the Queen to grapple with the daunting realities of pre-war tensions and diplomatic intrigue.

The white-clothed agent, a master of disguise and intrigue, known as the 'fake beggar', sat discreetly at the back of the Kaushambi hall. His mind was a whirlwind of thoughts, consumed with unravelling the intricacies of the construction project and its profound impact on the relationship between Magadha and Kalinga. Unlike his peers, he possessed a rare scepticism, questioning these two neighbouring people's stark differences in perception.

With piercing eyes and a straightforward demeanour, the agent delved into the ongoing project initiated by the Magadha administration - an ambitious endeavour to inscribe Maurya administrative principles on rock boulders surfaces across India. This initiative, driven by Pataliputra and a team of skilled carvers and sculptors stationed in Takshashila, aimed to disseminate bureaucratic ideals and reinforce public compliance through these rock inscriptions.

However, the project faced staunch resistance in Kalinga, a kingdom disconnected from Maurya rule and sceptical of Magadha's attempts to impose alien rules on its terrain. When Magadha sought to extend its inscriptions to Kalinga's hills and rock surfaces, the Kalinga Council of Ministers vehemently opposed it, asserting that Magadha had no authority over their natural landscape for such endeavours.

The rejection of Magadha's proposal was communicated back through Kalinga's royal messenger, a diplomatic act that inadvertently stoked the ire of Magadha's administration and military leadership. This event underscored the growing tension between the two kingdoms, with Magadha interpreting Kalinga's defiance as challenging its authority and prestige.

The agent noted that this incident had a lasting impact on the mindset of both Magadha and Kalinga's populace. For the people of Kalinga, it reinforced their perception of Magadha's overbearing and hegemonic attitude. At the same time, for Magadha, it fuelled anger and the desire to assert control over their neighbouring territories.

Amidst these geopolitical tensions, the 'face beggar' contemplated the more profound implications of this clash of ideals and its potential to exacerbate the brewing conflict between Magadha and Kalinga. His observations shed light on the intricate power, authority, and cultural sovereignty dynamics that defined the relationship between these two ancient kingdoms.

Tensions between the mighty kingdom of Magadha, known for its military might and strategic prowess, and the relatively peaceful kingdom of Kalinga, marked by incursions and displays of aggression along Kalinga's northern border, escalated. This sudden aggression from Magadha, a neighbour that had previously maintained a peaceful coexistence, was unprecedented, leaving Kalinga to rally its defences and unify in response. The kingdom of Kalinga, known for its rich cultural heritage and commitment to peace, had never faced such overt hostility from a neighbour that challenged its relatively peaceful rule.

In the face of Magadha's provocations, Kalinga mobilized its defence forces, including its skilled archers and martial experts, many Atavika warriors from the western tracts known for their swordsmanship and archery prowess. The *Atavikas,* deeply rooted in their martial lifestyle, joined with other areas under the Kalinga banner to defend their homeland with unwavering resolve. The spirit of patriotism surged across Kalinga, with resounding slogans throughout the kingdom proclaiming their independence and determination to resist any aggression from Magadha.

The news of Kalinga's united front and steadfast resolve reached Queen Karuvaki, sparking her curiosity about the leadership behind this wave of patriotism. She sought to understand who the king of Kalinga was and who the prominent figures were inspiring such enthusiasm among the people.

As the Queen inquired deeper into the situation, the

atmosphere became tense. Many agents and attendants around her wore expressions that hinted at deeper concerns. However, before she could delve further into these matters, an urgent summons from the Emperor interrupted her thoughts.

Upon reaching her husband's side, His distressed state struck Karuvaki. The Emperor, visibly troubled and overcome by fear, revealed that he believed the exact mysterious figure of the Kalinga battlefield, "the tall lady," had returned to this distant place and haunted him with unsettling questions.

This revelation shattered the Queen's heart, not because of any tangible presence of this "tall lady," which seemed impossible, but because it illuminated the depths of her husband's mental anguish and the torment he experienced from past events and memories.

The story unfolds against a backdrop of escalating tensions and personal struggles, highlighting the complexities of royal life intertwined with geopolitical challenges and the monarch's inner turmoil. The Queen's relentless quest for understanding and deep concern for her husband's well-being drove the narrative forward; ascend the intrigue and emotion amid the conflict between Magadha and Kalinga.

The interest in Kalinga over the rise of Prince Piyadasi, a man known for his ruthless ambition and lack of mercy, to the Magadha throne was deeply unsettling. News of the power struggle within the Magadha royal family, with reports of merciless murders and disputes among brothers, spread fear and apprehension throughout the kingdom. Karuvaki, as an eyewitness to these tragic events unfolding in Pataliputra, needed no reports or spies to understand the gravity of the situation.

As Kalinga people became increasingly aware of the brutality within the Magadha royal court, particularly Prince Piyadasi's ascent to power, they grew increasingly alarmed. The question of how a man who showed no mercy to his kin could be expected to govern with justice and compassion hung heavy in the air. The arrival of messages from Magadha's royal messengers, filled with veiled threats and ominous implications, only heightened Kalinga's anxieties, adding to the tension..

The Kalingadhipati, the king of Kalinga, stood as a beacon of defiance against Magadha's hostility. It was clear that Prince Piyadasi's administration sought compliance and complete subjugation of Kalinga. The Kalingadhipati's steadfast refusal to submit to Magadha's demands made him a direct enemy in the eyes of Magadha's ruler. Still, it also showcased the unwavering spirit of the Kalinga people.

Sarpa Mahamatra's solemn disclosure to Queen Karuvaki, a woman torn between her duty to her people and fears, highlighted the stark contrast between Kalinga's defiance and what might have been expected from Magadha in a similar situation. He suggested that the roles had been reversed. Magadha might have capitulated to the mighty neighbour rather than risk the consequences of defiance. This divulgence deeply affected Queen Karuvaki, leaving her visibly troubled and aggrieved by the implications.

Sarpa, recognizing the distress caused by his remarks, promptly apologized to Queen Karuvaki for any mental anguish inflicted. His words underwent the precariousness of Kalinga's position in any mental anguish inflicted. His words underwent the precariousness of Kalinga's position in the face of Magadha's aggression and the resolve of its people to resist subjugation at all costs. The unfolding events set the stage for a future fraught with tension and uncertainty between these neighbouring kingdoms, with Kalinga bracing itself for the looming threat posed by Piyadasi Raja and the ambitious Magadha administration.

Attack of the Mighty

Confined to her chamber, Queen Karuvaki was a vessel of apprehension, sorrow, and deep, unrelenting turmoil. The emissaries' disclosures of the brewing conflict between Magadha and Kalinga had cast a suffocating darkness over her thoughts. She was acutely aware of her husband, the Emperor, being consumed by a profound mental anguish likely intensified by the unfolding events in the region.

Her hands trembled as she contemplated burrowing deeper into the details of the unfolding disaster. The thought of the conflict, driven by imperial ambitions and selfish motives, filled her with dread. She harboured no desire for a greater Magadha built on bloodshed and conquest, knowing that such aspirations were antithetical to human values and conscience. Yet, she also understood the harsh reality of her world, where power and conquest prevailed over compassion and understanding.

Despite her reservations, Queen Karuvaki steeled herself to learn more, not out of a thirst for truth or awareness but of a desperate need to understand the source of her husband's torment. With deep-rooted compassion and understanding, she believed that the atrocities committed in the pursuit of imperial glory had shattered not only the land of Kalinga but also the hearts of its people and the natural beauty that had flourished there for centuries.

Summoning the espionage agent stationed in Kalinga,

the Queen took a deep breath, preparing herself for the worst news. She knew that whatever she heard would likely bring tears to her eyes, not just for the devastation inflicted upon her motherland but for the toll it had taken on her husband's fragile state of mind as the agents began recounting the events of the Kalinga War, the Queen's heart sank, her eyes welling up with tears. Each word painted a vivid picture of bloodshed, butchery, and cruelty. The scenes described were a stark reminder of the inhumanity that pervaded the pursuit of power.

Yet, amid the tales of horror and destruction, Queen Karuvaki's resolve to understand and support her husband grew stronger. She saw clearly that the consequences of such cruelty had paralyzed the Emperor's mind, leaving him broken and tormented. She also understood that these consequences extended beyond her husband, affecting the people of Kalinga and their way of life. This understanding fuelled her determination to bring about change and prioritize compassion and understanding over conquest and power.

At that moment, as she absorbed the grim details of the conflict, Queen Karuvaki vowed with a renewed determination to do whatever was in her power to bring solace and healing to her beloved husband, to mend his shattered spirit, and to mend the fractured relationships between their kingdoms. She knew that true strength lay not in conquest but in compassion and understanding.

A secret plot was brewing in the shadowed depths of Kalinga's dense southern forests. Sarpa Mahamatra and his spymasters stationed at Samapa came close and whispered to Queen Karuvaki about Magadha's clandestine military manoeuvres. The Kalinga War had simmered for a decade as an undeclared conflict, with Magadha continually probing and testing Kalinga's defences.

The Magadha War Committed launched a minor, exemplary attack to test Kalinga's response. Around two hundred cavalry soldiers would sneak through the dense forests of the south-western boundary, aiming to reach the coastal ports of Samapa and Palura, where Magadha spies were known to operate in large numbers. The aim was to surprise the enemy and quickly gain a foothold with minimal force.

Magadha's master tacticians instructed the Chief of Armed Forces, the Senapati, to approach Kalinga from the Avantiratha side, gathering young and agile cavalry soldiers for the mission. The plan was shrouded in secrecy, and success was anticipated.

However, fate had other plans. Their movements were detected as the Magadha cavalry traversed the main route towards the Mahakantara region, with the capital at Asuragarh. The secret had been maintained with utmost care. Unbeknownst to the Magadha forces, an unknown native soldier on leave from Avantiratha uncovered the undercover operation.

Arrow Stricken Avantiratha Cavalry

At Atavi capitals in western Kalinga, Asuragarh had vowed to defend against Magadha's incursions. Hundreds of archers waited with the vast bulk of arrows reserve, ready to unleash a rain of arrows upon the unsuspecting Magadha cavalry as they passed through the Narla dense forest towards Asuragarh.

Arrows pierced the air, claiming lives before they could reach even one yojana (seven miles) far from there. The Atavi retaliation was swift and fierce, driven by a longstanding rivalry with Magadha over gem and mineral mines claimed by Magadha.

The aware Atavi Chief of Asuragarh orchestrated the ambush without Kalinga's direct involvement, seeking retribution for Magadha's exploitation of their land's resources. The Avantiratha squads of Magadha left waiting for their cavalry soldiers were oblivious to the fate that had befallen the Magadha cavalry.

Queen Karuvaki, upon hearing of the debacle, maintained a stoic facade. Her mind raced with the thought of retaliation, believing in the principle of "tit for tat'. Though outwardly composed, her eyes betrayed a glint of satisfaction at the unexpected turn of events.

The aftermath prompted the Avantiratha provincial army to pass a confidential resolution to avoid further troop movement through the treacherous Mahakantara region. Magadha's costly loss was a stark reminder of the perils hidden within the intricate landscape of politics and warfare.

In the game of power and revenge, the southern divisions of Kalinga stood firm, sending a clear message that their lands would not be violated without consequence.

Queen Karuvaki sat in deep contemplation, her mind swirling with images of past battles and the weight of the one last month; she was unaware of the details. She sought answers amidst the turmoil, a longing to understand the fate of her homeland and its ill-fated ruler who faced the relentless onslaught of Magadha's formidable forces.

With its imposing elephantry, cavalry, and infantry, Magadha, boasting the mightiest battalion on earth, had become a looming threat to Kalinga. The spectre of war managers hired from far-away lands like Macedonia and Bactria adding their expertise to the enemy's arsenal deepened the dread within Queen Karuvaki's heart.

As she wrestled with these harrowing thoughts, a singular figure emerged- a name she could barely muster, yet whose destiny was entwined with the fate of Kalinga. The Toshali Raja, the unfortunate leader tasked with defending Kalinga against overwhelming odds, remained a shadowy figure in her recollections.

Slowly, in a thoughtful mood, she asked, "I do not hear anything about the King of Kalinga, and all of you have spent so long and searched so minutely the nook and corners of Kalinga. Enlighten me about the Toshali Raja; I was unaware of the unfortunate country chief once I was familiar with it. But my knowledge is meagre as I have been far away for so long, and the intervening relationship is not good."

Turning to his trusted agents, Sarpa Mahamatra summoned two shadowy operatives, the Black Leopard and the Canny Fisher, entrusted with intelligence from Toshali and the royal court. They approached the Queen, their whispers shrouded in secrecy, divulging details too clandestine for any other ears.

Listening intently, Queen Karuvaki processed the insights gleaned from the covert spies. She reflected on the ethos of her homeland, where nature and spirituality had once shaped governance - a stark contrast to the relentless administrative machine she had encountered in Magadha, where power, wealth, and authority churned incessantly.

In Kalinga, people revered a pious king advised by a council of regional chiefs, saints, wealthy merchants, generals acquainted with warfare and successful maritime *Sadhava* traders – a unique defence forged from unity and wisdom. The kingdom's roots in Jainism ran deep, with many saintly kings steering the realm during the dawn of this peaceful philosophy.

Recalling the last days before the devastating Kalinga War, Queen Karuvaki's heart ached for the saintly ruler burdened by the relentless cold war and undue stress. In a poignant moment of clarity, he dreamed of relinquishing the Crown to embrace the life of a Jain Arhat – a noble pursuit far removed from the brutal politics of the day.

Kalinga warrior scene 1

The Superpatriot of Kalinga – Mahasenani Bhaskarajyoti

With a sigh of relief, Queen Karuvaki found solace in knowing that the King of Kalinga had not succumbed to dishonour or defeat at the hands of Magadha. Though Kalinga faced untold suffering, the notion of a silent punishment inflicted upon the Toshali King offered a bitter-sweet reassurance – proof of the indomitable spirit of a kingdom unbowed, refusing to yield to an unconquerable enemy.

Amidst the turmoil and imminent peril, Kalinga, a kingdom steeped in a rich history of resilience and patriotism, found itself bereft of the physical presence of its revered king. Yet, veiled in secrecy and shielded by the unwavering loyalty of its people, the kingdom stood the tale of her homeland's resilience; her thoughts converged on the spirit of courage and sacrifice that permeated the land. She was attentive to what the spies were narrating.

The Black Panther's whisper carried tales of Kalinga's collective celebration of their king's departure – a departure not out of fear but of a profound commitment to safeguarding the kingdom's honour and sanctity. The king's absence was shrouded in mystery, known only through whispered rumours that spoke of his retreat for meditation. His return, eagerly anticipated, was the beacon of hope that kept the kingdom's honour - as today in modern Odisha, to conceal their beloved deity, Lord Jagannath, from Muslim attacks. The particular nature of society persists everywhere but is prominently seen in Kalinga and its geographical limits, whatever name it bears.

Then, the topic of discussion shifted to the proper subject.

Amidst the shadow of uncertainty, Kalinga's youth emerged as the vibrant heartbeat of the Kingdom – led by Bhaskerjyoti, the Mahasenani whose name blazed like the radiant sun. His robust presence embodied the essence of Kalinga's spirit, inspiring a legion of dedicated patriots to rally around the cause of defending their motherland. At the heart of this movement were many motivated youths, a beam of hope, and the epitome of Kalinga's resilience, who guided people with unwavering determination and a deep sense of duty.

Kalinga War

Dedicationof the Superpatriot and the Lay Public -

The streets of Toshali, the capital of Kalinga, were bustling with the energy of its people, and every corner of Kalinga, from the majestic palaces to the humblest of homes, reverberated with the resounding call of arms – alert for the motherland, a rallying cry that stirred the depths of every citizen's soul. From the seasoned warriors, their armour gleaming in the sunlight, to the ordinary folks, their faces etched with determination, a collective resolve took root, fuelled by a shared sense of duty and love for their homeland. The air was thick with the scent of anticipation and the sound of marching feet as Kalinga prepared to face its greatest challenge yet.

As the earth and sky resonated with the enthusiasm of patriotism, Kalinga's people forged an unbreakable bond, transcending age, gender, and profession. Their unity was not just a product of circumstance but a choice born of conviction, a determination to defy defeat and embrace heroic sacrifice to protect their beloved motherland. This unity, a shining example of their strength and courage, was the essence of Kalinga's spirit. The spirit resonates with any listener, and ignites a sense of solidarity, and inspires admiration for their unfaltering patriotism.

Queen Karuvaki, listening to the statements of the detective agents swept up in her people's emotional reactions, felt a surge of admiration for their unswerving and indomitable spirit. In their selfless dedication to the cause of Kalinga, she saw the embodiment of honour and unyielding defiance against the looming shadow of Magadha's aggression.

Amidst the echoes of war drums and the stirring chants of "Alert for the Motherland," Kalinga stood as a tall, sturdy wall of the enduring power of unity and patriotism – a hope amidst the gathering storm. And at its helm, Bhaskarajyoti, the flame of the Sun, led with calm determination, a symbol of Kalinga's steadfast resolve to face whatever fate the winds of war might bring. The looming shadow of Magadha's aggression, a formidable threat to Kalinga's sovereignty and way of life, added a sense of urgency and gravity to their struggle.

As the Black Panther's whispered narrative unfolded, Queen Karuvaki, a figure of strength and grace, found herself deeply moved by the bravery and unity displayed by Kalinga's populace in the face of impending peril. The kingdom was not gripped by fear; instead, it was galvanized into action, rejuvenated by a spirit of unshakable determination and solidarity. At this moment, Queen Karuvaki's admiration for her people swelled, her heart filled with pride for their courage and devotion to their homeland.

Amidst the urgency conveyed by Magadha's intelligence, Kalinga's Mahasenani, Bhaskarajyoti, a man of unparalleled strategic brilliance, emerged as a beacon of hope. His meticulous planning and foresight instilled a profound sense of ownership over their homeland. Kalinga was not merely a territory to be conquered; it was the cherished birthright of its people – a bastion of identity and heritage. His leadership, an exhibition of Kalinga's resilience, instilled a sense of reassurance and confidence in the locals, knowing their homeland is in capable hands.

Under Bhaskarjyoti's leadership, Kalinga prepared itself meticulously from the inevitable clash with Magadha's formidable forces. The youth of Kalinga, guided by a genuine desire to protect their land, orchestrated the evacuation of vulnerable populations and valuable assets to secure locations beyond Magadha's reach. The sea became a lifetime for families seeking refuge, arranged by brave maritime merchants and the spirited youth of Kalinga. The stage was set for a battle to test the mettle of Kalinga's people and their devotion to their homeland.

The Women and the Young Generation of Kalinga

Without Bhaskarajyoti, his wife, Chandravali, the tall Kalinga woman with a statuesque figure, she was stepped forward to lead the women groups of Toshali. Her presence fuelled the flame of patriotism, inspiring the young, robust youths of sound physique and under adult age to join the defence with ordinary weapons like sturdy and spiny bamboo sticks, ropes, and home weapons for self-protection. The active role of women in the defence of Toshali is a barometer of their strength and courage, empowering the readers and filling their hearts with pride.

The son and grandson of Bhaskarajyoti took the lead in the home at Toshali in organizing and motivating women and residents with assurance and courage.

The women folk did not opt to allow only their husbands, brothers and relations to die alone in the war. Still, they sacrificed themselves, inflicting the utmost damage on the invading Magadha infiltrators in the worst possible way. May he be the Piyadasi Raja!

They prepared the Toshali granary, a cruel source of sustenance for the invaders. They made it void and hid all the food material away from their sight and utility, ensuring that the enemy could not access to the food supplies. Kalinga felt the time of the year Magadha was invading, it was short of harvesting season; and the granaries were empty. The food reserves of Magadha Army will meet doldrums and performance of Magadha and hired Bactrian Forces to find the doldrums. The performance of Magadha and deployed Bactrian Forces will meet in ashes.

The Flame of the Atavi Land

Meanwhile, the Atavi Estates, stalwart vassals of Kalinga, and many forts in northern and southern regions mobilized their military capableness and industrial prowess to defend the realm. Each estate pledged its finest warriors and archers to strategic defence sites across Toshali. Ratnagiri Hills and the coastal regions of Samapa-Palura. The landscape was transformed into a labyrinth of natural obstacles – bushy trees, invisible ditches, trenches, and carefully positioned weaponry – all poised to repel any incursion by Magadha's forces.

The security preparations were shrouded in secrecy, unfolding in the isolated domains of the Atavi Estates beyond Magadha's surveillance. This clandestine defence would only come to light after the decisive battle, leaving Magadha stunned by the unexpected resistance and its staggering toll.

Queen Karuvaki, her heart swelling with pride, absorbed the tales of Kalinga's patriotic fervour and strategic brilliance. In Bhaskarajyoti and the committed lovers of Kalinga soil, she saw the embodiment of courage, sacrifice and firm devotion to their motherland. Theirs was a testament to the enduring power of unity and indomitable spirit of a people determined to defend their way of life against all odds.

As the Queen awaited the unfolding chapters of

battle, she searched for answers to the haunting agony that gripped her husband – a victory won against seemingly insurmountable odds, fuelled by the unbreakable resolve of a nation united in defence of its sacred soil.

In the shadow of impending conflict, Kalinga found itself in a precarious position, bracing for the aggression of a vindictive and powerful Magadha under the rule of cruel Raja Piyadasi. The rumblings of war had grown louder over the past eight years with warnings and annual intrusions. Magadha was proving increasingly aggressive and alarming with red eyes at the border. The relationship between Kalinga and Magadha, once marked by trade and cultural exchanges, had deteriorated over the years due to territorial disputes and political tensions. This, coupled with Magadha's growing ambitions and Kalinga's refusal to submit, set the stage for the impending conflict.

The Kalinga administration was baffled by how Magadha seemed to anticipate their every move and intention. Messages of warning and threats from the Magadha court reached Kalinga, demanding the cessation of any relationship with Atavi Lands, a strategic territory known for its rich resources and proximity to the influential Asuragarh in the Mahakantara region. They had been Kalinga's since the Mahabharata days. The Asuragarh, a fortress of great strategic importance, was a key point of contention between the two kingdoms. The messenger sent by Piyadasi Raja was detained in Toshali custody for days, only to vanish mysteriously, leaving behind ominous directives from Magadha.

The Council of Ministers in Kalinga was seized with urgency, as was the gravity of the situation and the imminent threat of a Magadha attack. The entire kingdom mobilized for war, with mass movements and preparations underway at all ports of Kalinga. Resources were swiftly imported from vassal territories like the Atavi Land, reinforcing Kalinga's defence in anticipation of the looming conflict. The Kalinga army, renowned for its discipline and bravery, was put on high alert. The people of Kalinga, from the youngest to the oldest, who were resident just before the war (leaving the mass moved for safety to Atavi security or overseas voyage), were trained in the basics of self-defence and emergency procedures. Every citizen was prepared to do their part for the sake of the motherland.

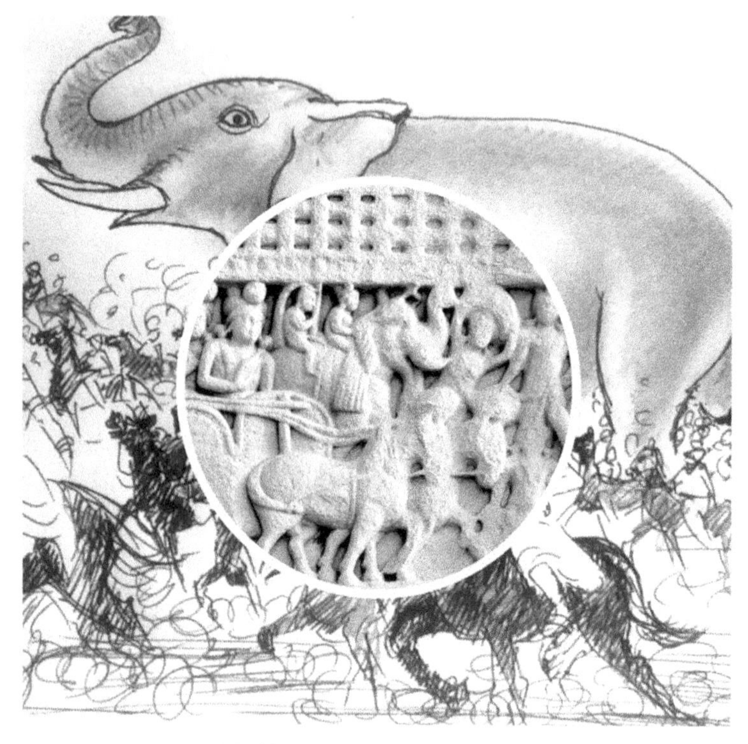

Kalinga War Emergency

Bhaskarajyoti, the Mahasenani and infinite source of courage, tirelessly motivated the populace to remain vigilant and resolute. His rallying cry, a symbol of the indomitable spirit of Kalinga, echoed across the land, inspiring a fierce determination not to yield to Magadha's threats. Bhaskarjyoti, a seasoned warrior and respected leader, was instrumental in organizing the Kalinga resistance. His unwavering belief in Kalinga's independence and ability to inspire others made him a symbol of hope and defiance. "**Kalinga can never bend to surrender but prefer to break after its last drop of blood is shed**," he declared, embodying the staunch spirit of independence and defiance that coursed through the veins of every Kalingan.

For the people of Kalinga facing war for the first time, negotiation and submission were alien concepts. They were not just proud of their land, ideology, and uncompromising spirit, but they held a deep-rooted belief in their freedom and sovereignty. The notion of obeying the commands of an enemy was inconceivable. Kalingans were straightforward and steadfast, unyielding in their belief that Magadha had no authority over their affairs and that their freedom and sovereignty were non-negotiable, a belief that commanded respect.

In the eighth year of the reign of the furious Piyadasi Raja, a profound sense of dread engulfed Kalinga as a formidable battalion of Magadha forces, like a dark cloud, established a camp along the Daya River, positioned in proximity to the south of Toshali settlement. This encampment was ominously timed just after the departure of clouds and rain when the flow of the rivers of the land was slowing down and was the autumn with yellow paddy fields with ripe paddy waiting to be harvested. But a camp of Magadha beside Toshali was looked upon by the Kalinga administration and populace as if one of the thatches among a row of such houses started to catch fire, minutes after it would engulf the whole settlement! The harvesters halted for their life was more precious than their one year's labour in yellow colour, the kingdom's agricultural bounty.

Magadha forces at the river's edge cast a pall of terror over Toshali and the surrounding regions. However, amidst the apprehension, with their firm determination, Bhaskarajyoti and his devoted group maintained a vigilant watch over every settlement. They adhered to a defensive strategy that prioritized readiness without provoking conflict until the main force of Magadha threatened Kalinga's boundaries.

The tension was evident, and the Council of Ministers, fully aware of the gravity of the situation, convened daily to deliberate on the kingdom's next step. Preparation was paramount, focusing on assembling the most agile tusker squadrons and deploying highly skilled archers to the forefront of defence. Ingenious strategies were devised, including positioning guerrilla groups to attack from behind enemy lines.

Each new morning they brought with it the spectre of impending battle. The people of Kalinga lived with the constant anticipation of conflict, with the Magadha battalion awaiting the arrival of their commander-in-chief, the formidable Magadha Emperor Piyadasi Raja. Kalingans steeled themselves with resolve, drawing motivation from their determination to withstand the cruelty of *Chandasloka*, whom they presumed to be a bloodthirsty demon of Indian epics.

Whispers spread among the populace, hinting that the dreaded Emperor had breached Kalinga's northern boundary, advancing forcefully into their territory. This ominous development further heightened the anxiety and resolve of the Kalingan people, who stood ready to defend their land and way of life against the encroaching menace of Magadha. Their hearts were heavy with the heat of the impending battle, but their spirits were steady, determined to protect what was rightfully theirs.

Kalinga found itself at a critical crossroads, torn between launching an attack on the Magadha camp or exercising patience and observing. The situation was amidst uncertainty and tension. Each with their perspective and wisdom, the councillors were engaged in a heated debate. Ultimately, they opted for a wait-and-watch strategy that showcased their bravery and strategic ideology. After all, Magadha had not officially declared war nor presented any proposal to Kalinga. Not even reiterated the term of surrender or amalgamation with Magadha. It was anticipated the alien party would first put forth the proposal and later move to any decision of war or quit. The Kalinga Council never expected a belligerent party to outright invade from the border, not camp beside the opponent's capital city.

Meanwhile, Bhaskarajyoti, the stalwart Mahasenani of Kalinga, anticipated potential retaliation. He dedicated his total capacity to monitoring the movements of the Magadha battalion. His steadfast commitment to Kalinga's safety, his sleepless nights and his tireless efforts were met with respect and admiration from his people. Rations to Magadha camp along the Daya River were abruptly halted, prompting unrest and unease among the occupants.

Behind the scenes, Kalinga's elephants and horses stood poised in hidden barracks nestled behind the hills to the west. Strategic units, led by seasoned commanders, were deployed to vital military roads, ready to impede the transportation of Magadha's war animals and equipment. The stage was set, and subtle but potent measures were implemented to deter the unwelcome guests on Kalinga's doorstep.

With its harvest ready paddy crops, the green natural Kalinga was a sight to behold, like a bride in her bridal

War Scene

dress, adorned with gold ornaments and exuding a pastoral charm. The blue sky and the song of the autumn birds created a serene atmosphere, while the fresh breeze carried the aroma of the ripe harvest, promising a bountiful year. With their transparent water, the streams and rivers evoked a primal thirst. This was the beauty of Kalinga, captivating and awe-inspiring.

But as Ashoka, the formidable ruler of Magadha, arrived with his entourage in the waning hours of a shady afternoon, the sky overhead was awash in hues of red and magenta – a haunting prelude to the dawn of a day that promised terror and bloodshed.

The resolute populace of Kalinga, accustomed to living amidst ferocious tigers and elephants, now faced a different kind of foe – a man whose cruelty rivalled that of the beasts. Yet, unlike wild animals, a man could be recognized by appearance, speech, or interaction. The gravity of the situation settled heavily upon Kalinga, revealing the harsh reality of confronting a king whose ambitions threatened their very existence.

The Kalinga War Diary

It was forecasted in the Magadha War Council that Kalinga would never stand for a confrontation with six times its strength and would surrender to the most significant power on earth in no time. But considering the forty years of resistance and the decade-long Cold War, the Kalingas together might defend the invasion of Magadha for hardly for two days.

Piyadasi Raja underestimated Kalinga's strength, and during his stay at the hillside, the military tents of Magadha Barrack would last hardly two days and three nights. He did not anticipate murders and bloodshed.

With the invasion from Magadha camps, Kalinga defended stalwartly, with elephantry taking the front. This caused a massive toll on the infiltrating, tired and half-fed Magadha infantry. The archers of Atavi Lands showered metallic arrows on Magadha Forces. It is natural for the local forces which are strongest on their home soil. Magadha had no answer at the outset. The hidden components appeared before they could realize the pros and cons.

Not all of the Maurya forces had yet arrived at their desired spots, which Kalinga natives well defended. Kalinga's wittiest war strategists anticipated a tri-fold attack. Pataliputra regiment arrived from north to Ratnagiri and Toshali; the Avantiratha troops from west to Samapa beside the Rushikulya River through a coastal route bypassing the treacherous Asuragarh track; the third, the Takshashila regiment reaching straight its Toshali target with their linear long-journey from far north-western India with many hired western war-giants and ghastly killing war weapons. They were delayed by a couple of days because the Emperor had some reasons to prepone the attack.

In this precarious moment, Kalinga stood as a steady mountain of courage and fortitude; with a gallant face each Kalinga, was applying his wit to possess the enemy, no matter the cost.

The Kalinga War, unleashed by the ruthless ambition of Piyadasi Raja, unfolded as an explosive clash with Toshali forces. Magadha has starkly a different approach from the classical followed Mahabharata style of war ethics with its formidable amalgamation of infantry, cavalry, and elephant units reinforced by foreign warriors skilled in Macedonian and Persian tactics, descended upon the fields of Toshali with the intent of mass-kill and conquer at all costs.

From the outset, the native Kalingan forces achieved overwhelming odds. Their prompt anticipatory preparedness had compelled a mass evacuation of a massive population to overseas or Atavi locations leaving behind only brave warriors who preferred to risk their lives in the rain of arrows on the battlefield. The toll of casualties mounted daily, with neither side relenting in their resolve.

The war, expected by Piyadasi, is swift and decisive instantaneously within two days, dragged on for one week, then two and thus many weeks marked by false declarations of impending victory like a wrestler falling and surviving. The Magadha forces, suffering increasing injuries and deaths, became hopeless and desperate. The foreign giant infantry of Bactria and Persia were helpless in the muddy and slippery battlefield and unaccustomed suburbs of Toshali, abandoned by residents. Several easy prey on ordinary Kalinga guards inflated the missing number from the foreign soldier camps. Finally, frustrated by the elusive Kalinga King and embittered by their loss, Piyadasi's commander cried for a brutal massacre, not on the Kalingan army but anybody anywhere, is it a baby, infant or an old, woman or man. Haunt at sight was the order approved by the watching Commander-in-Chief, Piyadasi, and the brutal king.

Every evening Piyadasi dreamt of the war's end and his conquest by tomorrow evening. Still, tomorrow was shifted every evening due to one plea or another – Magadha Forces faced new and new challenges every day and confrontations varied from secret guerrilla attacks at camps battlefields to their armoury or reserve food. When the Kalinga guerrillas spoiled the Western hired troops with acute perception the tamed Kalinga tuskers misled the opponent's war elephants, weeks extended to many. They even surpassed the Mahabharata 18 days' war on the open Indraprastha battlefield. It was all due to miscalculations and inexperience in the geography of Kalinga.

There was no way that Magadha's straightforward victory would have been achieved with vast mass of forces. What they followed was a descent into barbarism – a campaign of slaughter that extended beyond the battlefield into the very homes and streets of Toshali and its suburbs. Women, children and people were easy prey: it was accompanied by crop destruction and setting fire to every thatched village and accumulated harvested paddy heaps. The unforeseen event charred a green kingdom into ashes, a land of horror and despair.

But every evening Piyadasi, unaware of the Kalinga

King's presence or absence, turned red with anger when he heard the Mahasenani, Bhaskarajyoti was a solid barrier in the war. His tactic strapped the forces on the battlefield and the devastating units in the suburbs and countryside. The genocide operation of Magadha was also equally suicidal due to the wit of the Mahasenani.

His marshals failed to capture the Mahasenani, Bhaskarajyoti, even with the announcement of a thousand gold coins award over his head. Magadha's troops were terrified when learned of his attack. Piyadasi was hopeless in confronting the Kalinga King, seen nowhere, and was gloomy with the valiant defence displayed by Bhaskarajyoti.

For a day short of one week, Piyadasi was harassed by news of Bhaskarajyoti's damage to the hired troops. It was a shame to Magadha in the international sphere and he was particular about saving every hired soldier. He was puzzled every evening by news of the war spies. He was so desperate, was hopeless and thought of quitting the battle.

Amid this carnage, a pivotal realization dawned upon Emperor Piyadasi. As the news reached him of the death of Bhaskarajyoti, Piyadasi's rage turned inward as he contemplated the atrocities committed in his name.

The Kalinga superpatriot's demise followed the deaths of his son and grandson on the Daya riverside battlefield. The father could not bear the murder of his son and grandson on the twenty- second day of war and met his fate.

The Magadha Senapati's revelation that the Kalinga King was nowhere to be found shattered Piyadasi's facade of conquest. Enraged and demoralized, he abruptly halted the bloodshed, recognizing that he had been waging war against children and women – a kingdom of peace-loving people who had suffered unspeakable horrors at his command.

He asked his conscience whether the Kalinga War was virtuous or sinful. "Sinful, sinful, sinful!" his conscience shouted back.

"No, no, no! I must visit the riverside to estimate the death and the ill fame of Piyadasi, the sinner," he thought and rose to the riverside with his two bodyguards.

Triple Attack

Amidst the devastation, humanity began to stir within Piyadasi's conscience. He questioned the virtue of the Kalinga War – realizing, with a profound sense of guilt, that it was an act of profound sin. In a moment of clarity, he acknowledged the gravity of his misdeeds, denouncing the war as a violation of '*Dhamma*' – the righteous path.

Instantly, he realized he had committed every sin in the Kalinga War. His aspiration to lead a righteous life and perform good deeds for a better afterlife seemed futile. He was consumed by '*Dharma Vaye*' – the fear of wrong deeds overshadowing his pursuit of righteousness. Restless and thoughtful; he condemned himself for his grave misdeeds, a betrayal of '*Dhamma*'.

Piyadasi then envisioned retrospect and prospect. His conscience halted, and a black flash closed all his prospective conjectures. He knew the present world and the afterworld and the truthful way of availing it through religious and honest means. He had every reason to debar from his march on the lines of 'Dhamma' which was what he had been doing the last few years, the biggest blunder is the mass killing in Kalinga.

He had 'Dhamma Vaye' – tremendous fear on religious grounds and talked to himself, "My retrospects show me a deed of '*Adhamma*', opposite of what is right. I must stop here, beg apology, and close the battle chapter."

By the time the superpatriot Bhaskarajyoti died following his son and grandson, his wife came to the spot and collapsed and died; her spirit was revengeful to the Piyadasi Emperor for his cruelty. The spirit had a way of punishing the culprit through her supernatural appearance. She carried the emotions of the woman-race of Kalinga facing the demise of spouses, destruction of families, and torturing humanity.

Beside the river, in the shadows of remorse, Emperor Piyadasi knelt in repentance. Burdened by the gravity of his sins, his soul sought forgiveness from the heavens, vowing to amend his ways and embrace the principles of humanitarianism and righteousness. As he opened his eyes, a statuesque figure appeared before him – a symbol of conscience and redemption, beckoning him to rediscover his humanity amid the ruins of the war.

The bodyguards already narrated the events that followed with the appearance of the tall Kalinga woman, the statuesque already known to Queen Karuvaki. She could have glimpses of what happened there and the identity of the tall Kalinga woman possessing her husband.

This assessed the course of the battle and the Emperor's role and responsibility in it. She was afraid that no god, no man, or living being would appreciate what her husband had done. No Emperor could appreciate the truth and rightfulness of Piyadasi's deeds.

The Queen could visualize the war in her mind's eye and squatted down there, deep in thought how to recover her husband from such heinous crime.

Kalinga War Ended

The Restitution of Guilt and Remorse

Accurate details about the Kalinga War, narrated by the divine force within the rock elephant, bewildered Kalu and Budu, who were silent for some time. They were proud of what their ancestors could do, and their mood was ecstatic.

"Are we the proud descendants of the worthy race!" exclaimed Budu.

"Sure, the portrayal by the divine power configures it!" expressed Kalu.

They started a little earlier today with long strides. With each step, they anticipated the impact of the Kalinga patriots and the many Kalingans who taught a vital lesson to the bloodthirsty Magadha Emperor. The air was thick with suspense as they neared their destination their heart pounding with the thrill of the impending revelation.

Their conversation had not ended, and they found themselves at the foothill of Dhauli. Then, they reached the rock elephant, completed the rituals, and waited patiently for the story to unfold.

The rock elephant started whispering in a clear tone.

In the aftermath of the devastating Kalinga War, a conflict that saw Magadha Emperor Piyadasi lead a brutal campaign against Kalinga patriots, he found himself haunted by the spectre of his actions, tormented by guilt and regret. His mind was a tumultuous sea of conflicting emotions, his soul a battlefield of remorse and self-condemnation. The war had left a deep emotional scar on him, a scar that was perceptible to those around him yet remained unspoken and deeply internalized. Meanwhile, Queen Karuvaki, attuned to her husband's suffering, sought to provide solace and distraction, aware that the scars of war lingered in his mind. Her efforts to comfort and guide him towards recovery proved the transformative power of faith and compassion.

One day, Karuvaki attempted to divert the Emperor's thought by drawing his attention to the serene sight of boats sailing across the Yamuna River beside the Kaushambi palace, where they stayed during the Queen's elicitation of espionage detail.

Unbeknownst to her, this innocent gesture triggered a traumatic reaction in Piyadasi. His mind, still entangled with memories of the Daya River stained with blood, plunged into a distressing illusion. The simple mention of a red boat amidst the flow of river traffic transported him back to the horrors of Kalinga, causing him to writhe in anguish.

Recognising the depth of her husband's trauma, Karuvaki resolved to shield him from recent unpleasant memories. She avoided locations with a view of the river and remained cautious about broaching topics related to Kalinga or the war. She did this not out of fear or ignorance but out of a deep understanding of his pain. She focussed on providing comfort and experience, allowing Piyadasi the space to grapple with his inner demons without external pressure.

In the silence of the night, the Emperor's troubled mind surfaced once more, revealing his hallucinations and haunting visions. He spoke of a tall lady from Kalinga, a spectral guide urging him towards *'Dhamma'*—the path of righteousness and contentment. Yet, Piyadasi remained entrenched in self-doubt, lamenting the enormity of his sins and the moral complexities of his actions. These visions, a manifestation of his inner turmoil, were evidence of the transformative power of his spiritual journey.

Karuvaki, ever supportive, then sought to assuage her husband's guilt by affirming his dedication to his kingdom and his people. She painted his conflicts as a means to a noble end – promoting the welfare of his subjects. In her understanding, she hoped to soothe his troubled spirit, steering the conversation away from the stark realities of war and towards a narrative of redemption. Her role in his journey towards recoupment was pivotal, her understanding of the events arousing confidence in the Emperor to confront the inner demons.

The Emperor's struggle continued, marked by moments of clarity and introspection, as he grappled with the weight of his decisions. Karuvaki remained steadfast, offering silent support and firm compassion, navigating the delicate balance of acknowledging the past while nurturing hope for the future. Her role in his journey towards recovery was crucial, her understanding and support providing him with the strength to confront his inner demons.

The Emperor's struggle continued, marked by moments of clarity and introspection as he combated the weight of his decisions. Karuvaki remained firm, offering silent support and uniform, steady compassion, navigating the delicate balance of acknowledging the past while nurturing hope for the future. Her role in his journey towards recovery was crucial; her understanding and support provided him the strength to confront his inner demons.

In the aftermath of the devastating War, a conflict that left a trail of devastation and death, Queen Karuvaki navigated the delicate terrain of her husband's troubled conscience with dedicated devotion. As she sought to extinguish the fiery embers of his preoccupation with the war's devastation, Karuvaki drew inspiration from the profound teaching of Mahabharata. This timeless epic was woven with the curtains of life's struggles and moral dilemmas.

Addressing her husband's deep-seated anguish, Karuvaki reflected on the epic's wisdom, likening Piyadasi's journey to a divine incarnation to alleviate the earth's suffering in her view, the Emperor had endeavoured to mend the fractures wrought by conflict, much like the mythical heroes of ancient lore.

Yet, Piyadasi's heart was ablaze with inner turmoil. His tearful confession laid bare a deep-seated fear of mirroring Duryodhana—Mahabharata character, consumed by greed and moral blindness. The weight of his sins against innocents and a defenceless kingdom burdened his conscience, threatening to drown him in a sea of despair. His journey towards healing was a tumultuous one, a journey that mirrored the timeless struggle of epic heroes, navigating the complexities of virtue and vice, retrieval and forgiveness.

Queen Karuvaki, a firm pillar of support, saw a path towards absolution through divine intervention. She spoke of seeing blessings from Lord Shiva, a deity renowned for his transformative power and capacity to cleanse the soul. Yet, Piyadasi's heart remained heavy with doubt, scarred by past rejections from religious factions during his ascension to the throne. His struggle with donation was palpable, but Karuvaki's stable faith in him never fluctuated, inspiring him to keep seeing his spiritual path. This path led him to a meeting with a revered representative of Buddhism, an ideology that had begun to resonate deeply with Piyadasi in recent years, offering him a new perspective and a chance for spiritual rejuvenation.

Undeterred, Karuvaki turned towards a new approach, suggesting a meeting with a revered representative of Buddhism—an ideology that had started to resonate deeply with Piyadasi in recent years. The teachings of Buddha, once foreign to him, now held the promise of solace and spiritual renewal, bridging the chasm between earthly turmoil and celestial excellence.

As Karuvaki orchestrated these moments of solace and reflection, she guided Piyadasi through meditation and prayer, encouraging him to confront his past and seek forgiveness. The Emperor was burdened by his actions, yearned for absolution and a path towards inner peace; his journey mirrored the timeless struggles of epic heroes, navigated through the complexities of virtue and vice, recovery and forgiveness. It was a journey that held the promise of spiritual renewal and transcendence, illuminating his hope amidst the darkness of his past.

In the sanctuary of their shared experience, Karuvaki's steady devotion guided Piyadasi towards the possibility of spiritual renewal. Her love for him was the driving force behind his transformation, proof of the power of her lovingness.

In the serene beauty of Kaushambi, where the echoes of Buddha's wisdom still lingered, Emperor Piyadasi embarked on a profound journey. His soul was wracked with torment and of deep yearning for peace. Karuvaki, his dedicated wife, orchestrated a poignant meeting with a venerable *bhikku* from the grandest Buddhist monastery in a desperate bid to heal the Emperor's deep wounds and guide him towards spiritual healing.

The venerable *bhikku,* a living repository of Buddhist wisdom and compassion, listened as Piyadasi recounted the harrowing tale of the ill-fated Kalinga War and the profound wounds it had inflicted upon his conscience and spiritual *mise-en-scene.* Drawing from Buddha's teachings, the *bhikku* gently illuminated the principles of ahimsa (non-violence) and righteous conduct that form the bedrock of the Buddhist way of life.

The Emperor, tormented by his intense fear of '*Dhamma*', a concept that had haunted his nights since the War, was in internal turmoil. The tall woman on the battlefield, always charging in terms of '*Dhamma*' or righteousness, accused him of an '*Adhamma Raja*' of Magadha. This 'Adhamma' threatened to strip him of his virtue in his eternal life, his life in the next world, and curse his progeny with all sorts of evils of life.

At any cost, at any strenuous worship, the Emperor wanted to earn virtue and virtue instead of punishment for sin. Both the Emperor and the Queen asked the *bhikku* whether they could tide over the '*Adhamma*' committed by the Emperor. The *bhikku* well-versed in spiritual texts and teachings, was seen as a guide in the Emperor's quest for redemption.

The learned *bhikku* confronted the royal couple with a soothing and reassuring presence. He assured them that in Buddha's teachings, it is indeed possible to transition to the '*Dhamma Path*', leaving the '*Adhamma*' behind, offering a glimmer of hope in their dark times.

He invoked the example of Bimbisara seeking the Buddha's counsel, emphasizing the importance of compassion, lawful conduct, and filial piety in the governance of a righteous ruler. The *bhikku*'s words resonated deeply with Piyadasi, who realized the stark contrast between his role in the War, a conflict that had left him spiritually wounded, and the ideals espoused by Buddhism.

Embracing the profound teachings of Buddhism, Piyadasi embarked on a path to recovery—a journey marked by introspection and profound transformation. The *bhikku* illuminated the transformative power of *moksha,* liberation from the burdens of sin through dedication and spiritual practice. He outlined the duties of a Buddhist ruler, envisioning Piyadasi as an example of *Dhamma,* righteousness and compassion, a ray of hope for his people.

Under the bhikku's tutelage, the Emperor embraced the role of an *Upasaka*—a devoted lay disciple committed to propagating the teachings of Buddha and fostering the culture of *Dhamma* among his subjects. The prospect of spiritual renewal infused the Kaushambi palace with optimism leading to mental healing, and Piyadasi's newfound commitment to compassion and righteous conduct that began to appear in his governance.

As Karuvaki witnessed her husband's metamorphosis, a renewed sense of optimism for their future blossomed within her. The Buddha faith had become the rays of the rising the sun after a dark night. The Emperor's hope was illuminated towards forgiveness and inner peace. As the palace resonated with vigour, enthusiasm, and happiness, Karuvaki's support and her role as a pillar of strength and understanding catalyzed Piyadasi's journey of spiritual rejuvenation.

In the gentle embrace of Buddhism, Piyadasi embarked on a sacred odyssey—an odyssey defined by enlightenment, compassion, and the redeeming promise of *Dhamma*. Through the *bhikku*'s guidance, he found the courage to confront his past transgressions, seeking forgiveness from Buddha and absolution from the burdens of his tumultuous reign. Once overburdened by the radiant promise of Buddha's teachings and the transformative power of righteous living.

As the tranquil rhythms of Kaushambi echoed the melody of spiritual renewal, Piyasasi's heart swelled with gratitude, encouraged by the radiant promise of Buddha's teachings and the power gained by Piyadasi to renovate himself. And amid the serenity of their sanctuary, Karuvaki and Piyadasi embraced the dawning of a new chapter—a chapter imbued with the timeless wisdom of Buddhism and the external quest for inner harmony.

As the Emperor, burdened by the haunting spectre of '*Adhamma*'—the shadow of unrighteousness cast by the Kalinga War—Karuvaki embarked on a relentless quest for '*Dhamma*'. This was not just a quest to guide him towards the luminous path of '*Dhamma*' through the teachings of Buddha, but a deeply personal struggle for recovery. This intensely personal and yet universal struggle, resonating with the evolving potential of Buddha's wisdom, led Karuvaki to envision a pilgrimage to Pataliputra—a vibrant nexus of Buddhist spirituality and enlightenment.

In Pataliputra, the epicentre of Buddhist practice and evolution, Karuvaki sought solace and sanctuary for her ailing husband, whose troubled conscience yearned for dismissal from the '*Adhamma*' of his tumultuous administrative decision—a decision that led to the suffering of many. The city pulsated with the rhythm of monastic life; its labyrinthine alleys were adorned with towering monasteries and the devout presence of revered *bhikkus*.

In the royal household, nestled within the rich

tapestry of Buddhist ideology, Karuvaki, a beacon of wisdom and devotion, played a pivotal role. She bore witness to the Emperor's nephew's indelible influence—a genuine Buddha disciple and an ardent proponent of the '*Dhamma*'. Under his tutelage, Karuvaki witnessed and guided a profound metamorphosis unfolding within the depths of Piyadasi's soul—a metamorphosis that would pave the way for spiritual renewal and enlightenment.

As the palace walls resonated with Buddhist practice's sacred chants and contemplative serenity, Piyadasi and Karuvaki embraced the prospect of spiritual rejuvenation with firm determination. The *bhikkus*, custodians of Buddha's timeless wisdom, extended their benevolent embrace to the Emperor—a troubled monarch seeking refuge in *Dhamma*'s sanctuary.

In the tranquil embrace of Pataliputra, amidst the auspicious ambience of Buddha's teachings, Piyadasi and Karuvaki embarked on a sacred odyssey—a transformative journey guided by the principles of righteousness, compassion and profound introspection. Each step towards enlightenment heralded a departure from the shadow of '*Adhamma*' illuminating a path towards spiritual emancipation and divine grace.

Under the watchful gaze of Buddha's benevolence, the Emperor found solace and recovery. Once burdened with the weight of sin, his heart now glowed with the promise of '*Dhamma*'. Guided by the devotion of Karuvaki and the profound wisdom of Buddhist teachings, Piyadasi underwent a profound transformation. He shed the shackles of the past, embracing a new legacy defined by righteousness and enlightened governance.

Buddham.Saranam.1

In the hollowed precincts of Pataliputra, Piyadasi and Karuvaki stood united— a testament to the transformative power of faith and the eternal quest for inner harmony. As the city resonated with the melodies of spiritual renewal, the Emperor's troubled soul found sanctuary in the luminous embrace of '*Dhamma*' – the enduring legacy of righteous living.

Kalu and Budu were happy with the Emperor's genuine and daily deepening entry into '*Dhamma*', or Buddhism. They also praised Karuvaki, the Kalinga daughter, for her continuous motivation and assistance in the Emperor's journey towards humanity.

As the story of the day ended, they started to return home.

The New Upasakas

The exciting part of the story was taking its shape. The heartless person on earth was blessed with a heart. It may be an incredible matter, but it started happening. The story listeners of the rock elephant could realize the truth. The sorrow of the massacre is a permanent scar in the mind of the Emperor, only to be erased after his material end. But all efforts were on to make it fade from memory. It was well-known to the original Hindu mind, and the effect of *karma,* deed, and the after-birth concepts of *Vedas* and *Puranas*. It was the internal candle fire of apprehension of the Emperor's mind. He had not been able to order as a king boldly, but was docile and almost mute on circumstances. None on earth had witnessed this part of the story. Still, his Proclamation, which can be surely a possibility of his '*Dhamma Vaya*', the fear of righteousness and the imagination of future life and the '*Yama-Danda*' or the punishment awarded in hell by the *Yama,* the God in charge of death in *Sanatana Dhamma.*

The story listeners were well aware of this basic religious philosophy. They appreciated the facts elaborated by 'Seto', the white rock elephant, an impartial witness and keen observer of the pages of history. The tale is the contemporary material experience with the divine eyes that have its field of vision on the whole of the earth since its creation. It did not include the fabricated the material, which was far from reality, and it witnessed the preparation of the rock edicts from editing to inscription stages. But the rock elephant had a doubt: were the rock edicts so meticulously inscribed that ordinary people of the country read the script made by the costly sculptor inscription team? Few people could have read the script, and a few literate royal interpreters were posted on the edict sites to announce the Proclamation.

The visitors were curious about the edicts' utility since they were so boldly inscribed on boulder surfaces at pilgrimage sites. The rock elephant also answered the sad story that the edicts' purpose never fulfilled Emperor Piyadasi's ambitions, who had spent his time and energy so frantically after this job. His team, no doubt, had been active since his tenure, and after his tenure, the Maurya Empire collapsed within decades. Ages and rulers passed on, and even within five centuries, the Brahmi script was forgotten due to lack of use and the descriptions lay in Greek and Latrine on Indian rocks. Many monarchs felt the gravity and grandeur of a mighty king and his ambitions from the artifacts and edicts but without his name and aim bearing the traces of Buddhist ideology. Archaeologists could decipher it only two millennia after its making, and the process is still ongoing.

Still, one doubt sometimes tides at the mind's shore, the story of Karuvaki. This rock-edict Queen was the lucky Queen Consort and the second queen. Where is her Kalinga origin? When did she marry the Prince Piyadasi?

Budu spoke, "No doubt, she was our Kalinga's '*Charubhasi*', the princess with a musical tone. She was the daughter of a vassal king of Kalinga, the kingdom around the Baitarani River basin. The king was a great mariner and merchant who settled in the past middle age as a ruler and Member of Kalinga's Council of Ministers. He had his residence at Toshali. These are not written documents, but the legends and folk tales elaborate the deep-seated regional feelings in the Baitarani base pre-Mauryan Buddhist settlements developed after the two disciples of enlightened Buddha, Tapasu and Bhalika, built stupas with Buddha's gift of a tuft of hair. Nowadays many awards and trophies have been named after Karuvaki. Many institutions also bear the name of the Queen Consort of Piyadasi. "

"Indeed, my dear friend. I have a question—was Piyadasi already married to her before Kalinga War? Some narratives portray her as a war captive of Piyadasi who later became his wife," Kalu inquired, sparking a speculative discussion.

Budu responded with conviction, "That was my initial understanding. However, upon reading the Queen's Edict issued by Piyadasi at Kaushambi, now relocated to Prayagaraja, considering the name and possible age of Prince Tibal as an adult, I am inclined to believe that Piyadasi and *Charubhasi* of Kalinga (*Charubhasi,* later in Pali language, was called Karuvaki) became life partners a decade before the Kalinga War and even before anointment. It is likely that Karuvaki witnessed the family disturbance and gave birth to Tibal before the war. Kalinga's wealth and culture might have enticed Piyadasi."

"I admire your presumption and mental mathematics. I had the same calculations but fumbled to speak out boldly as you have expressed", replied Kalu, who was more knowledgeable than Budu from historical and tourism point of view. His tone was respectful and appreciative of Budu's insight.

Their conversation ended when they arrived at the

Dhauli Hill base. They worshipped the rock elephant and sat down before Seto, concentrating on listening.

Seto, the rock elephant, was cheerful and started its story.

As the Emperor concluded his initial meeting with the monastery monks, a sense of relief washed over him, marking the beginning of a new chapter in his spiritual journey.

"How far did you have faith in Buddha before yesterday?" asked the Emperor to Karuvaki.

"Indeed, my Master, My faith in Buddha has been steadfast before our union," the Queen affirmed, her firm support shining through her words.

"But I took it superficially. A girl of Kalinga and daughter of a marine merchant, I had little belief that you could be a disciple of the Great One," mocked the Emperor for the first time in the last six months.

As the monks, representatives of the Mauryan Empire's official religion availing royal support and maintenance, departed, Emperor Piyadasi and Queen Karuvaki found themselves in a profound conversation. This marked a significant moment in the Emperor's life. At this moment, his stoic facade began to crack, revealing a man deeply moved by the Queen's faith and devotion, a faith deeply rooted in the teachings of the Buddha that had been gaining popularity in the empire. This was a turning point in the Emperor's perception of the Queen's faith.

Emperor Piyadasi, intrigued by the depth of Queen Karuvaki's faith, discussed her beliefs. Her response was not just a personal testament but a reflection of Kalinga's rich cultural heritage, a heritage deeply intertwined with the teachings of Buddha.

In a moment of light-hearted banter, the Emperor

remarked on his initial scepticism regarding Karuvaki's affinity for Buddhism, reflecting on the unexpected nature of their union. They had come from different backgrounds, with the Emperor being a staunch follower of the Mauryan religion and Karuvaki being a devout Buddhist. However, Karuvaki gently reminded him of the profound connection between her homeland of Kalinga and the early disciples of Buddha, Tapasu and Bhalika, emphasizing the rich spiritual heritage that had shaped her beliefs.

The Emperor's tone softened as he absorbed Karuvaki's sweet words, recognizing the inherent wisdom and spirituality present in her upbringing. He acknowledged her kingdom's unique strengths and resources, admiring its harmonious relationship with the world of nature and its innovative approaches to sustainability.

Proposing a new vision for their partnership, the Emperor expressed his desire for Karuvaki to serve as his trusted advisor, guiding him to promote their people's welfare and the society's greater good. He acknowledged the importance of having a loyal confidante who could help him navigate the complexities of governance and decision-making, a role he believed Karuvaki was uniquely suited for, given her wisdom and devotion.

Proposing a new vision for their partnership, the Emperor expressed his desire for Karuvaki to serve as his trusted advisor, guiding him to promote their people's welfare and the society's greater good. He acknowledged the importance of having a loyal confidante who could help him navigate the complexities of governance and decision-making, a role he believed Karuvaki was uniquely suited for, given her wisdom and devotion.

Karuvaki, deeply honoured by the Emperor's trust and confidence in her abilities, pledged her firm support and loyalty. She embraced her role as his aide, committed to assisting him in every endeavour and ensuring the success of his reign.

Inspired by the Buddha's teachings, Emperor Ashoka shared his vision for a society steeped in compassion, kindness, and enlightenment. His vision was not a utopian dream but a progressive and radical idea for his time. He envisioned a world where the profound wisdom of Buddhism was not just a privilege of the elite but a guiding light for all, leading them to a deeper understanding of life's purpose and meaning. His vision included social reforms, such as the abolition of slavery and the promotion of animal welfare, that were radical for his time.

Ashoka, Karuvaki – Buddha Saranam

Karuvaki wholeheartedly embraced the Emperor's noble aspirations, recognizing the transformative potential of spreading the teachings of the Buddha far and wide. She affirmed her commitment to helping realize his vision, understanding that their partnership would be instrumental in shaping the destiny of their kingdom and its people. Her insights and understanding of Buddhism played a crucial role in shaping the Emperor's vision, a fact that was not lost on him.

As they shared their hopes and dreams for the future, Emperor Piyadasi and Queen Karuvaki united in purpose, bound by a shared dedication to truth, compassion, and enlightenment. Their commitment was a deep-rooted conviction that would guide their every action. Together, they embarked on a journey to bring about positive change and create a legacy that would endure for generations.

Emperor Piyadasi, his psyche deeply scarred by the Kalinga War, undertook a profound emotional journey. In his darkest moments, he found solace and guidance in the teachings of the Buddha. His past indifference towards Buddhism, which now seemed like a veil that had been lifted, revealed the profound wisdom in the Buddha's words. The suffering he witnessed in Kalinga tore open his heart, exposing him to the raw truth of Buddha's teachings, and he felt an unbreakable bond with the Enlightened One.

Moved to tears by the compassion and forgiveness espoused by the Buddha, Emperor Piyadasi recognized the profound significance of the Buddha's presence in his life. He saw the Buddha as a beacon of hope and solace, sent by the divine to alleviate his mental anguish and provide him with the guidance he desperately sought.

Queen Karuvaki, a steadfast pillar of strength in the Emperor's life, keenly observed his inner turmoil. With her words of solace and profound insight, she became a ray of hope for him. She reminded him that forgiveness was the noblest form of revenge, urging him to forgive himself for the suffering he believed he had caused. She underscored the transformative power of embracing the Buddha's teachings, illuminating the path to inner peace through compassion and forgiveness.

In response to the Emperor's inquiry about his royal duties about Buddhism, Queen Karuvaki suggested a path of active engagement and spiritual practice. She proposed that the Emperor could become a strong *Upasaka*, or lay follower of Buddhism, actively supporting and promoting the teachings of the Buddha in his kingdom.

Emperor Piyadasi enthusiastically embraced the idea, his heart aflame with newfound purpose. He recognized the potential for meaningful action and spiritual growth within the framework of Buddhism. He expressed his determination to engage with Buddhism as a passive supporter and an active participant, dedicated to upholding its principles and values in every aspect of his life and rule.

With a renewed sense of purpose and resolve, Emperor Piyadasi vowed to seek guidance from the esteemed monk Moggaliputtatissa (also addressed as Upagupta) and explore how he could best serve the cause of Buddhism. He expressed confidence in his ability to leverage his talents and resources for the benefit of the noble religion, eager to fulfil his role as a faithful disciple of the Buddha.

"Now I am again calling for the great monk to my palace. We three will take some time, and I have my skill and intention so agile within me, you don't know. I am not the Emperor of Magadha only; I have my appreciation in different directions not disclosed to any. I hope my favoured talent will be quite helpful for the noble religion.

I will disclose it before the monk judges its utility," the solemn Emperor said.

"Now I feel Lord Buddha lives in you. He must find us the best path that we will choose. His saffron-coloured *kasaya* represents purity, and making it pierce the spectator's mind is a promising and fulfilling ideology. Mogalliputtatissa is Buddha today and will show how you can move following the Great Light of the dark life," said the Queen satisfactorily, her belief in the Emperor's potential shining through her words.

As the day of Moggaliputtatissa's long-awaited visit to the palace approached, Emperor Piyadasi's heart swelled with eager anticipation. The monk's arrival was not just an event but a moment that would shape the trajectory of his reign. The Emperor, a mix of excitement and reverence, personally received the messenger who carried the monk's letter, fully aware of the profound impact this communication would have on the propagation of Buddhism.

Despite his advanced age, the saffron-robed monk radiated a youthful energy and a wisdom that transcended time. His mere presence commanded respect and admiration, and his serene demeanour was evidence of his compassion, a living embodiment of the Buddha's teachings.

Humbled by the monks' presence, the Emperor greeted him with a profound reverence, acknowledging Buddha's profound impact on his life and reign. Recognizing the monk's spiritual authority, the Queen Consort paid her respects, bowing at his feet in reverence.

In their private conversation, the Emperor expressed his profound remorse for the violence and suffering of past conflicts, acknowledging his duty as a ruler to seek redress for his subjects' grievances. He shared his vision of promoting Buddhism as a path to peace and enlightenment, seeking the monk's guidance and blessing in his noble endeavour.

Moggaliputtatissa, recognizing the sincerity and earnestness of the Emperor's intentions, offered words of encouragement and wisdom. He affirmed Buddhism's transformative power to alleviate suffering and promote harmony, urging the Emperor to continue his pursuit of spreading the Buddha's teachings far and wide.

Moggaliputtatissa, a revered monk and disciple of Gautama Buddha, had taken it upon himself to enlighten the Emperor with the timeless wisdom contained within the '*Dhammapada*', the collection of verses spoken by Buddha. With a few good enchanting monks, Moggaliputtatissa held a spiritual '*Dikshya* Ceremony' for the Emperor with original chants of '*Dhammapada*'. As the words from heaven, the Emperor got into the original sayings of Buddha that purified his heart and soul. With deep reverence and dedication, Moggaliputtatissa spent seven days imparting the principles of Buddha to the Emperor, guiding him along the path of peace, compassion, and self-awareness.

Emperor Piyadasi was astonished by the profound simplicity of Buddha's teachings, particularly the emphasis on wisdom not derived from mere verbosity but from inner peace, love, and fearlessness. He reflected on the Buddha's words, recognizing the importance of embodying these qualities.

Taking the five precepts of Buddhism to heart, Emperor Piyadasi pledged to abstain from actions that caused harm to others, including taking life, stealing, adultery, lying, and intoxication. He understood that violating these precepts would only lead to suffering in this life and the next.

'Buddham Saranam'

However, the deeper spiritual insights within the *Dhammapada* truly stirred the Emperor's soul. He was moved by the teachings on cultivating goodness, avoiding evil, and purifying the mind. The realization that 'true victory lay not in conquering others but in conquering oneself' is the outcome of Buddha's versions sensitively impacted his psyche.

At this juncture, the tall Kalinga woman with a figure of a statuesque was standing in the left upper corner of his mind's screen, Buddha in the middle teaching his human virtues. In the subset picture, the tall woman indicated her finger; Buddha right through the ages and in the afterworld that you feel after causing a disaster to humanity. Now you admit humanity is the essence of creation, a vital force of nature and the nidus of life right through the ages.

Haunted by the memory of the tall Kalinga woman and burdened by the gravity of his past actions, the Emperor grappled with a newfound sense of humility and introspection. He knew fully well his inhuman destructive deeds were drowning him in the ocean of humanity, but the sermons may not neutralize his sins, yet a drowning man catches at a straw. He has no other alternative. He realized all his deeds from the spirit of the battlefield, the Kalinga woman.

He began to see himself as a mere instrument of fate, subject to the divine will of *Dhamma*. The revelation that Buddha had foreseen his actions filled him with awe and a deep sense of responsibility, for which he underwent a profound transformation of heart and mind as he grappled with these truths. He accepted that he was destined for a greater purpose than his past transgressions and that redemption was within his reach through embracing the teachings of *Dhamma* with sincerity and humility. This realization, this transformation, was nothing inspiring.

With a renewed sense of purpose, Emperor Piyadasi made a solemn vow to dedicate himself to the path of righteousness and compassion, guided by the timeless wisdom of Gautama Buddha. As Kalu and Budu listened to the tale of the rock elephant, they, too, felt the stirring of something deep within their souls. They felt a connection, as if they, too, were being beckoned to embark on a journey of self-discovery and spiritual awakening. This journey was not exclusively for the Emperor but was open to all.

Buddham Saranam Gachhami

Now, Moggaliputtatissa had to propose a saintly name for Buddhism, which ignited Piyadasi Raja.

The Emperor, encouraged by the monk's words, sought his permission and expertise in a bold endeavour: publicly confessing his faults and proclaiming his commitment to promoting Buddhism throughout his kingdom and beyond. He expressed his readiness to utilize all his resources and influence to make Buddhism accessible, seeking the monk's guidance in this notable endeavour.

As the Emperor awaited the monk's response, Moggaliputtatissa's face seemed to glow with an inner radiance, reflecting the depth of his spiritual insights. He considered the Emperor's proposal with a serene demeanour, recognizing its potential to bring about profound change and transformation in the kingdom.

Their conversation marked a pivotal moment in the Emperor's spiritual journey as he sought the guidance and blessing of one of Buddhism's most revered monks. Together, they envisioned a future where the principles of Buddhism would guide the Emperor's reign, bringing peace and harmony to all his subjects.

With a sense of anticipation, Emperor Piyadasi prepared to unveil his innovative strategy for spreading Buddhism to Moggaliputtatissa. The monk and Queen Karuvaki, sensing the Emperor's excitement, listened intently. The Emperor hinted at a remarkable device that could revolutionise the dissemination of Buddha's teachings across his kingdom, transcending the barriers of social status and case.

As the Emperor began to unveil the technique, Moggaliputtatissa's curiosity was piqued. He was eager to learn more about his mysterious device that could potentially change the course of Buddhism. The Emperor started with the historical significance of Takshashila, the capital of the northern Maurya province, Gandhara. It was renowned for its stone architecture and the prestigious Takshashila University.

Emperor Piyadasi recounted a pivotal moment in history when his grandpa Chandragupta Maurya with Vishnugupta, also known as Chanakya, the Acharya of Arthashastra, Politics and Economics in Takshashila University and ex-officio Chief Advisor of Maurya Emperor decided upon the upgrading the University; they requested the University to have one innovating wing among its twenty-two arts and crafts education, the rock and rock inscription wing. This ground-breaking initiative brought together artisans from interdisciplinary segments and fostered a dynamic exchange of ideas and languages, leaving an indelible mark on the history of Buddhism.

Deeply inspired by the Emperor's foresight, Moggaliputratissa marvelled at the potential of this resource for spreading Buddhism. He proposed the creation of a small editorial group to craft inscriptions for rock edicts strategically placed in areas frequented by tourists. Pillars, sculptures, and motifs would complement these inscriptions to captivate and inspire the readers. The Emperor's enthusiasm was palpable as he personally oversaw the crafting of pillars with lions, the strong animal four in a bunch, elegant elephants, bulls, and many domestic creatures, all designed to attract people.

During his Takshashila stay as a prince, he was interested in innovative stone crafts. He knew very well the scripts available in western Aramaic language, newly-recovered native Brahmi scripts with an intermediary local script of Gandhar, the Kharostri types. Many Buddhist Acharyas of the university had produced bunches of artisans making Buddha in stone, stone surfaces and inscribed Buddha's sermons on scripts and symbols.

The monk suggested that the Emperor should bear the name, *Devanampiya Piyadasi,* or the "Beloved of the Gods". This new Buddhist name was intended as a popular name for any Proclamation. Addressing him as *Devanampiya Priyadasi* will make him a true disciple of Gods, Buddha and the Truth. This will erase all his past inglorious deeds. Inscribing any other name he bore will be a hindrance to hiding his inhuman actions. This was a lesson for the editorial board and the sculptors.

Thus, the new title was accepted and embraced by the Emperor. It was a title imbued with authority and reverence, and he expressed deep gratitude for the monk's sage advice. The gravity of the title stirred memories of the Kalinga War and the haunting presence of the tall woman, but the Emperor's acceptance of it showed his humility and respect for the monk's guidance.

That vulnerable thought of the moment could be read from the face of the Emperor by none other than Karuvaki. She provided comfort and reassurance, urging him to focus on the present and the opportunity to alleviate suffering through his actions. With renewed resolve, Emperor Piyadasi and the Queen Consort bid farewell to Moggaliputtatissa, grateful for his guidance and inspired by the path ahead.

As the monk bid farewell to the palace, his heart swelled with contentment and sadness. He knew his counsel had been received with sincerity and gratitude, and to the Emperor's satisfaction, the monk was a true disciple of Buddha's greatest reward. Yet, he couldn't help but feel a pang of longing, for the opportunity to sow seeds of compassion and wisdom was a privilege he cherished.

The rock elephant, a masterful storyteller, completed the best portion of the story and was delighted. Both the listeners were quite happy and curious to ask how august it was when such events occurred on earth, events quite similar to Buddha's enlightenment.

The rock elephant sighed at the question and replied, it was some years before the sculptors arrived here to dig me out of the hill. Even by this time, the Kandahar Rock Edict facing the west in Aramaic scripts and Macedonian language with story of the Kalinga War was completing its ninth year of commission. Artisans, carvers, and sculptors of West and Gandhar were part of the academic platform of script carving and linguistic exchanges. The local Royal

Maurya Prince and the Dhamma Mahamatra of Toshali stationed here after prevail of Maurya administration were the prime coordinator for construction of mine out of the mass of the hill stone.

The listeners were astounded by the rock elephant's exceptional memory, clearly demonstrating its unique storytelling talent that left them in awe.

'Dhamma', 'Dhamma' and 'Dhamma'

Emperor Ashok's transformation from a ruthless conqueror to a zealous *Upasaka* (a dedicated Buddhist layperson) was entirely a personal journey. It marked a profound shift in his reign and legacy, a change that occurred approximately one year and a half after the devastating War. This Conflict had shaken Ashoka to his core, leading him to seek solace and guidance in the teachings of Buddhism. Immersed in the *Dhammapada* and Buddhist scriptures, he redirected his royal energies from hunting and merrymaking to religious pilgrimages, embarking on a monumental journey of spiritual and ethical reform.

Karuvaki was captivated by Emperor Piyadasi's steady devotion to Buddhist principle. She witnessed his daily immersion in religious activities, consistent chanting of Buddha's practices, and dedicated efforts to propagate these principles among the people. His commitment to simplifying the dissemination of Buddhist teachings through rock edicts was truly inspiring, as it brought the profound wisdom of Buddhism to the masses, regardless of their diverse languages and literacy levels across Jambudvipa (India).

Rock Edicts

The Emperor's vision, shared with Karuvaki, was not just a dream but the dawn of consciousness among the masses. It painted a future where Buddhist propaganda would grace tourist sites and settlements across India. His belief in this widespread exposure to Buddhist teachings, even among the non-worshipper of gods, was not just a wish, but beginning of a new era to further enrich the already. This vision, born out of his deep understanding of the power of *Dhamma*, instilled a sense of optimism in those who heard it.

Karuvaki was full of admiration for the Emperor's humility in his initiatives. She commended that his prime

Edict, proclaimed at Kandahar, reflected the significance of his confession regarding the Kalinga War. This act of humility, she believed, would humanize him in the eyes of his subjects. The Emperor's sensitivity in ensuring that the Kandahar Edict was not visible to the people of Kalinga was a well-planned mindset out of his guilty thoughtfulness and respect for his humane feelings ushered late in his life span.

Emperor's Plans for Kalinga were not just about establishing a monument but a promise to symbolize compassion and benevolence. His description of how local artisans, along with Persian sculptors, would craft and image of the Seto or white elephant—a representation of *Indradeva*'s divine mount—from the rocks of Dhauli Hill was a proof to his deep concern for the welfare of the orphaned and widowed villages of Kalinga. This evoked a strong sense of empathy and understanding for his actions.

The Emperor's concern for Kalinga moved Karuvaki. She recognized the healing touch of such a project would have on the region's reconciliation. The Emperor's plans included establishing schools, hospitals, and welfare centres in the area, which she knew would provide much-needed services and symbolize his commitment to the welfare of his subjects. She acknowledged the Emperor's humility in attributing the endeavour's success to Buddha's mercy.

As the Emperor prepared to meet with the editorial team to draft more edicts, Karuvaki marvelled at his enthusiastic dedication to spreading the message of *Dhamma*. She knew that his efforts would not only shape the future of his kingdom but also leave a lasting legacy of compassion and enlightenment for generations to come. The Emperor's interactions with the editorial team were characterized by his openness to diverse perspectives and his commitment to ensuring that the edicts effectively communicated the principles of *Dhamma* to all sections of society.

Queen Karuvaki's support of Emperor Piyadasi's religious journey was not just a passive act but a powerful force that provided him with the positivity and encouragement he desperately needed to enthuse his inner turmoil. Despite the challenges, she remained steadfast in her commitment to fostering a positive atmosphere around the Emperor, ensuring no negative thoughts could breach his mental sanctuary. Her role in this transformative period was truly admirable. As the Emperor delved deeper into the teachings of Buddha, he found solace in the sermons of Moggaliputtatissa (his other name is Upagupta), whose constant commitment to Buddha's teachings was a wellspring of inspiration. With each passing day, the Emperor's fascination with religion grew, and he eagerly absorbed the wisdom and philosophy of Buddha. His heart yearned for pilgrimage to sacred sites such as Saranath and Lumbini, where the spirit of Buddha still resonated.

During his royal expedition, the Emperor consciously shifted the focus from activities that harm to animals, such as hunting and sacrifices and dedicated his time to visiting sacred sites and spreading the teachings of Buddha. His actions set a powerful example for the entire Maurya kingdom, leading to the abolition of the once-common practice of animal sacrifice under his decree. He prohibited the *Samaja* and *Utsaba,* the celebrations involving animal slaughter.

Queen Karuvaki rejoiced as she witnessed the Emperor's transformation into a devout follower of Buddha. During one year and a half following the War, he emerged as an esteemed advocate for the Dhamma, tirelessly promoting Buddhist principles and erecting pillars and inscriptions to spread the message of *Dhamma* far and wide.

Their son, Tivara, wholeheartedly embraced his parents' devotion to Buddhism, joining his mother in supporting his father's spiritual journey. Together, they chanted the refuge formula, seeking solace and guidance from the Buddha, the Dharma, and the Sangha. Their collective devotion created a bond of unity and love that transcended earthly realms.

Dhamma, Dhamma, Dhamma

Piyadasi's pivotal decision to inscribe his edicts at religious and essential tourist spots revolutionized the dissemination of *Dhamma* (moral law), Buddhism, and humanitarian principles throughout his empire. Jambudvipa, the ancient native term for the Indian subcontinent, was transformed into a vast canvas for Piyadasi's moral philosophy. His inscriptions, etched on rocks, pillars, and other prominent structures, aimed to foster a righteous and harmonious society by promoting ethical conduct and compassion.

Piyadasi's vision of *Dhamma* extended beyond the confines of Buddhism. Aware of the diverse beliefs within his realm, he crafted a universal moral philosophy that could unify his subjects. This *Dhamma* emphasized respect for all life, obedience to parents and elders, and reverence for *Brahmanas* and *Sramans*was a call for compassion, non-violence, and moral integrity that transcended religious boundaries. His compassion for all life was a guiding principle in his rule.

The Emperor enlisted the finest architects and artisans from Gandhara's renowned rock industry to ensure the widespread dissemination of these principles. These skilled craftsmen created inscriptions adorned with intricate carvings of animals, bulls, elephant, lions, and more – designed to capture the attention and imagination of his subjects. The visually striking edicts were strategically placed to ensure that the messages of righteousness and civic duty reached every corner of the empire.

Karuvaki was thrilled by her husband's attempts, not because he excelled in his sphere because of the height he attained in grasping what Buddha told and the practical application of Buddha's ideology. Still, his covered mind by the clouds of memory was being released to a brilliant sun in the sky. She never ventured to ask him about his mind or any instance of Kalinga.

"What else can we do for Kalinga," Piyadasi often shouted at Karuvaki. But intentionally she avoided proceeding in Kalinga direction. Any discussion she feared would arouse the sleeping tiger of depression in the Emperor's mindset.

But when Karuvaki heard that the Emperor was setting up some big establishments at Ratnagiri and the Baitarani valley, sending his kith and kin and the most prospective Buddhist monks, she was mentally pleased. Some religious revolution was entering her birth place that would be prominent for centuries. But she never expressed her appreciation or pleasure for such a show. She was sceptic about whether the remote memories of Piyadasi would arise.

Simultaneously, administrative reforms were on line, transforming in a novel way in favour of the subjects. Piyadasi's love for his subjects was akin to that for his offspring, rather than mere tax-payers. He appointed divine administrative assistance in the administrative apparatus, the *Dhamma Mahamatras,* the religious officers dedicated to promoting moral and ethical conduct throughout the empire. These officers were responsible for embedding the principle of *Dhamma* in every facet of society, from family life to public administration, ensuring the well-being of his subjects.

Amidst this religious fervour, a sense of homely warmth enveloped the palace, fostering a bond of spiritual unity and familial love that transcended earthly realms. The Emperor's relentless pursuit of religious enlightenment inspired all those who crossed his path, leaving an indelible mark on the fabric of Mauryan society.

Queen Karuvaki, a witness to the profound transformation of her husband, Emperor Piyadasi, known to history on Ashoka was filled with awe and admiration. The Emperor's journey into Buddhism was not just a change of belief but a profound personal transformation. He not only embraced the teachings of Buddha but also infused his entire palace with the spirit of Sangha, creating a sanctuary of spiritual enlightenment. His vision extended far beyond the borders of Magadha as he aimed to spread the message of *Dhamma* to distant lands, echoing the words of Buddha that his teachings would reach the unreachable Tamraparni and endure for millennia. Emperor Piyadasi was a visionary. He envisioned a world where the principle of non-violence and humanity would prevail, radiating from Pataliputra to the farthest corners of the earth. His emissaries were dispatched to Tamraparni, Suvarnadvipa, the Far East Isles, and even the distant lands of Macedonia, Persia, and Bactria, carrying the call for compassion and enlightenment. His role in preserving Buddhism cannot be overstated.

Despite the passage of almost two centuries since the time of Gautama Buddha, Buddhism thrived under Ashoka's reign, buoyed by royal patronage and financial support. However, the Sangha was not immune to challenges. Non-Buddhist monks sought to distort its actual teachings, posing a threat to its integrity. Ashoka was distraught when he received information about the crowding of the Sanghas by non-Buddhist residents on the pretext of availing from the luxuriant royal alms to the Sanghas.

He planned to do something; otherwise, Buddhism would have the only fate of degeneration and disintegration. He called upon the most erudite monk, his mentor, Moggaliputtatissa and solicited his way of intervention, "*Bhante*, can you suggest to me how to specify the Sangha for pure Sanghians, the torch bearers of Buddha?"

"Yes, Your Highness, Emperor Devanampiya Piyadasi, it is the abundance of your alms that corrupts the system of the erstwhile Sangha, and the infiltrators have pleasure in consuming the redundancy and showing their presence by chanting sermons not transmitted by Buddha in his *Dhammapada* It is appropriate time to identify the infiltrators and remove them away," replied the great monk.

Ashoka then turned to his mentor, Moggaliputtatissa, to learn how to reform the Sangha and purge the uninvited elements. This context sets the stage for the Third Buddhist Council.

Recognizing the urgent need for reform, Ashoka and Moggaliputtatissa convened together the Third Buddhist Council. This was not just a gathering but a pivotal moment in the history of Buddhism. The Buddhist Council was convened to enact reforms and regulations to preserve the purity of Buddha's teachings. It marked a significant milestone, ensuring that the essence of the *Dhamma* remained untainted for future generations.

Amidst his religious fervour, Emperor Ashoka embarked on a pilgrimage to the birthplace of Buddha at Lumbini, a journey that was deeply personal and profound. He had previously erected structures in honour of the Enlightened One at this holy site. With a decade of devout practice as a "*Striving Buddhist*" under his belt, Ashoka had approached this sacred site with a keenness born of deep reverence and spiritual longing, seeking to walk in the footsteps of the ascetic prince who had renounced worldly pleasures to seek enlightenment.

The conscience of the Emperor was active enough to appreciate the gratitude he owed to his better half, Queen Karuvaki who spent her heart and soul for his well-being. She had selfless dedicated service for him, not only consoling him but showing him the righteous path that Buddha focussed by his torch.

In a serious mood, as always, he was disposed then; he had some humour with Karuvaki. "You are a torch bearer to me besides my religion. I must edit the drafts of the inscriptions and you will appear in all the rock and pillar edicts now on make," was a smiling story for her.

The Queen turned grave and mute, looked to the Emperor's face.

In the serene halls of the imperial palace, the Emperor and his devoted aide were engrossed in a profound discussion. They were deliberating over including her name in the monumental edicts that would disseminate the teaching of *Dhamma*. This spiritual philosophy had recently taken root in the Maurya empire, far and wide across Jambudvipa. This was a critical moment in the history of the empire, as the Emperor sought to immortalize Queen Karuvaki's contributions to the spread of Buddhism. The religion started gaining popularity rapidly. However, the humble Queen expressed her reluctance to be singled out in such a public manner, a unique character of a Kalinga princess, sighing and reluctant face to appear in the forefront, now the powerful Queen Consort of the world's most powerful dynasty, a symbol for humility and devotion. Her humility was addition to her selflessness and dedication.

A heart heavy with conflict, Queen Karuvaki earnestly implored the Emperor not to raise her above the family, choosing to remain a nameless figure in the grand design of the mandates, meant for royal officials and public. Her struggle with her modesty and devotion was palpable in her words as she respectfully declined the Emperor's offer.

Her soul was torn between the desire to be recognized for her contributions and the fear of overshadowing her family. Her struggle is a scene to expose the complexity of human emotions and the moral dilemmas one faces in such situations.

Emperor Ashoka, fully aware of Queen Karuvaki's pivotal role in his spiritual journey, saw her as a symbol of dedication and selflessness. Her decision to decline his proposal demonstrated the proof of her commitment to their shared path of enlightenment, a choice he deeply respected and admired, further strengthening their bond.

Emperor Ashok proposed a compromise in a gesture of profound respect and love. He spoke out, "Alright, my dear. The honour and reward you deserve for your dedicated services in the spread of Dhamma, the people of this locality, Kaushambi, where the Maurya dynasty and even myself, Ashoka Raja, identified by your presence, people will misunderstand us, the makers of the pillars and the posts in skipping your benevolent services availed by them. You can't remain aloof from the proclamation programme: you hold the key of all donations and transactions in religious dissemination."

He suggested localizing her presence in the Kaushambi pillar which needed to be inscribed in the edited document. Kaushambi was a place of sacred significance where they had sought refuge during turbulent times. This compromise symbolized his deep understanding of her wishes and profound expression of his love for her. His empathy and love for her were evident in this compromise.

Queen's Pillar, Kaushambi (now displaced)

Yet, despite the Emperor's earnest attempts to honour her wishes, Queen Karuvaki remained pensive and reserved. Her thoughts turned to their son, Tival, whose burgeoning potential and future inheritance weighed heavily on her heart. She silently prayed for his well-being and guidance, her motherly emotions intertwining with her steady devotion to their family and the teachings of the Enlightened One. Her love for her son and her dedication to her family was as strong as her commitment to *Dhamma*'s teachings, and this balance defined her character.

In the quiet interlude of their exchange, amidst the echo of their shared convictions and aspirations, the bond between Emperor Ashoka and Queen Karuvaki blossomed, a credential of their unity in purpose and steadfast commitment to the noble ideals of *Dhamma*.

Despite his profound remorse for the suffering caused by the Kalinga War, Ashoka's affection for Kalinga was enhanced, with a secret will to repay the loss by kind words, religious temperament and accepting the people of Kalinga as kith and kin. His intention to construct me, the Rock Elephant was out of his deep desire to religiously grant the vision of a heavenly creature, which was ominous in the incarnation process of Lord Buddha. The white elephant of his mind was the purest celestial creature, even not less pious that the *Dhammapada* recitations of Saugata Buddha. His temperament, awed by the thought of the havoc was prompted to compose the special Kalinga Edict, which outlined the regional fostering programmes. Even though the Yuvaraj (Crown Prince) stationed at Toshali and the Mahamatra at Samapa were tasked with Governing Kalinga, the extensive inscription throughout the region spoke volumes about Ashoka's deep-seated commitment to its well-being.

The rock elephant, Seto, is a timeless monument to Ashoka's enduring connections to Kalinga. Carved shortly after his remorse found ways of dissipation, the process of transformation and dedication to Dhamma, the idea of Buddha's birth had impressed his thought of the first divine ray of Buddha's presence, the dream of Airabata white elephant by mother Maya Devi. The divine spell within Seto resounds as whisper, the truth of Ashoka's journey, a narrative that will never fade from the pages of history.

As Kalu and Budu absorbed this profound narrative, they understood that Ashoka's Dhamma was more than a moral code; it was a heartfelt expression of his repentance, his desire to heal war wounds and his commitment to building a compassionate and just society. The rock elephant's tale revealed the depth of Ashoka's transformation, offering a powerful lesson in the enduring power of remorse, redemption and moral leadership, inspiring all who hear it.

Both the story listeners were not in a pose to bid goodbye to Seto, who could speak so much from the dark, unseen, and unheard-of facts from days of yore, not even shaped in the pages of history. Budu was so curious he did not accept that Seto had completed the story.

He requested Seto, "Kindly Divine Guru of ours, we are eager to know the last days of Emperor Ashoka and Karuvaki and his terminal days. A divine soul, spending a major part of life as the reaction to his remorse, how was his life?" The audience, like Budu, was filled with curiosity and anticipation for the rest part of the story.

Seto whispered, "Sure, we were only on Kalinga's perspective. Ashoka's long days of making the rock and pillar edicts involved a vast apparatus spreading the whole of India. His hectic schedule guiding his editorial staff and inspecting and inaugurating one or more monuments monthly spent away most of his lifetime. New ideas were entering into the process, and he was busy with his *Dhamma* transmission outlook. I understand your curiosity. We will take our last part next time on his last legs."

They returned to their village road hoping to come next Wednesday to quench their thirst for antiquity with the continuation of Seto's tale.

On the Last Legs

Twenty-four monsoons had gone by, each leaving its mark on the world around him. As time flowed relentlessly onward, Emperor Ashoka reflected on the passage of seasons and life cycles. The lush green flora remained unchanged, reminding him of nature's resilience. For the Emperor, life journey had taken him through a profound transformation, from the innocence of youth to the weight of kingship, a journey that shaped his character. His struggle with the past and his efforts to make amends were a testament to the impact of his responsibilities on his character..

Despite his relentless efforts to atone for the sins of his past through the propagation of Dhamma, a complex concept encompassing moral and ethical principles and acts of benevolence, a shadow of regret persisted within Emperor Ashoka. The memories of Kalinga, the battlefield stained with blood and sorrow, continued to haunt his thoughts. His quest for forgiveness and solace in the teachings of the Buddha was often overshadowed by the spectre of his past deeds, leaving him in a state of inner turmoil. This internal conflict, this battle within, is a testament to the depth of his struggle and the sincerity of his recovery.

The Emperor's beloved Karuvaki, his constant companion and guiding light of life, was no longer by his side. The weight of her absence bore heavily on his heart, her voice now a silent echo in the chambers of his mind. Had she ever extended an invitation to visit Kalinga to confront the ghosts of his past? The unanswered question lingered, a testimony to the depth of their connection and the void she had left behind, which was once filled with her steady support and love. Karuvaki, a symbol of his earthly attachments, had played a significant role in his spiritual journey; her absence was now a constant reminder of the impermanence of life and the need for inner peace.

In the depths of his soul, he wrestled the ghosts of his past and the tall woman of Kalinga, a symbol of the lives lost and the suffering caused by his actions. This woman, a representation of Kalinga's collective anguish, had a profound impact on Ashoka's spiritual journey, a constant reminder of the consequences of his past actions and the need for recovery.

Yet, amidst the turmoil of his inner struggles, there was a glimmer of hope. The Emperor's steadfast commitment to the path of righteousness and tireless efforts to spread the message of peace and compassion stood to his enduring faith in the power of recovery. As he stood amidst the towering pillars of his empire, inscribed with the sacred words of *Dhamma*, the Emperor sought solace in the teachings of the Buddha. With each passing day, he moved closer to the elusive goal of inner peace, his spirit uplifted by the eternal promise of forgiveness and salvation.

As the sun dipped low on the horizon, casting a golden glow over the serene landscape of Dhauli Hill, Seto, the rock-cut white elephant built by Emperor Ashoka, stood as a witness to the final moments of the Great Emperor's life. With a solemn air, Seto reflected on the tumultuous journey of the Emperor, from the heights of conquest, where he expanded his empire with brutality, to the depths of remorse and cure, where he was haunted by the horrors of war and sought solace in Buddhism.

Reasons lying within humanity, the Emperor had no will to visit his most sacred creation at the base of Dhauli, but Seto was sure he must be wishing and praying the Buddhist divine he had set within him here. If he intended to visit, the tall Kalinga woman must be behind his mind, shadows echoing, 'Where are you going once again?"

Gazing upon the edicts that adorned the nearby pillars, Seto pondered Ashoka's legacy, a man whose life was a collage woven with threads of conquest, remorse, and spiritual awakening. With a voice imbued with wisdom and compassion, Seto began to narrate the poignant tale of the Emperor's last moments:

'I have fought many battles, but the greatest war was within myself,'

Ashoka's voice echoed in Seto's retelling, capturing the depth of his introspection. This 'tumultuous journey', a metaphor for the ups and downs of his life and his internal struggles, was a crucial part of Ashoka's spiritual transformation, leading him towards recovery and inner peace.

Seto spoke of Ashoka's inner turmoil, the weight of regret and sorrow that had burdened his soul since the fateful days of the Kalinga War, a brutal conflict that claimed countless lives and left the land soaked in blood. Despite his efforts to atone for his past transgressions through the propagation of Buddhism and acts of benevolence, Ashoka carried the scars of his actions deep within his heart.

As Seto recounted the Emperor's agony, tears welled in his stone eyes, mirroring the sorrow that gripped Ashoka's soul. He spoke of the Emperor's solitude in his final days, bereft of familial companionship and facing the inevitability of his mortality. The scene was set in a simple chamber adorned with symbols of Buddhism, where Ashoka spent his final moments in quiet contemplation. In these moments, Ashoka's spiritual journey reached its culmination; his inner struggles and quest for redemption finally derived solace from the teachings of the Buddha.

But amidst the sombre reflections, Seto also spoke of Ashoka's firm devotion to Buddhism, the guiding light that had led him from darkness to light. Despite the trials and tribulations, Ashoka found profound solace in the teachings of the Buddha, seeking refuge in the Three Jewels—the *Buddha*, the *Dhamma*, and the *Sangha* till his last breath. The Three Jewels, the core principles of Buddhism, played a crucial role in Ashoka's spiritual journey, guiding him towards inner peace and satisfaction.

Dhauli Collage

In the twilight hours, as the air grew still and the world seemed to hold his breath, Seto's voice resonated with a profound reverence as he recited the sacred words:

"I surrender to the Buddha for refuge.

I surrender to the *Dhamma* for refuge.

I surrender to the Sangha for refuge."

With these timeless words echoing through the hallowed grounds of Dhauli, Seto stood as a silent witness to the passing of a great soul, his steadfast presence a monument to the enduring legacy of Emperor Devanampiye Piyadasi, popularly known to the world as Ashoka, the Beloved.

[Dhauli Shanti Stupa]

End Notes:

Human minds often exhibit an iceberg phenomenon when it comes to tragic events, be it rooted in science, the supernatural, or the decipherment of an illegible ancient inscription. Such an instance occurred during archaeological explorations in India and Odisha, where a colossal war transformed a ruthless Emperor into an ideal proponent of peace and harmony. This king, who was once a murder-minded *Chandashoka* and perpetrator of one of the most dreaded wars of his time, the Kalinga War, emerged as the embodiment of virtue. The transformation of Emperor Ashoka, from a brutal conqueror to a champion of peace, is a fascinating journey that invites deep exploration. While concrete evidence of this war may be scarce, the rock inscriptions left by the Emperor in the most remote corners, away from Kalinga, strongly suggest the occurrence of a bloody conflict. Present-day inhabitants, who once identified as Kalingans and now as Odias, may grapple with accepting the gravity of this evidence. The sheer numbers involved may seem unbelievable, yet architectural remnants attributed to this tyrant Emperor are tangible reminders of the tumultuous past.

When a curious mind delves into an issue, it navigates through the vast expanse of history and geography, weaving number of possibilities intertwined with deciphered facts. Event after event unfolds, shaping the narrative of ancient stories from the Dark Ages. Scholars with profound knowledge dissect and analyze through their specialized lenses, while the inhabitants who dwell in the very locations where these stories are rooted possess a unique temperament - a willingness to embrace the potentialities and likelihoods, a perspective that only a Kalingan or an Odia can truly understand.

Historians meticulously scrutinize events, poets weave narratives, and the locals, rooted in the region's soil, perceive the past through a lens of accepted possibilities. The darkness of ages doesn't obliterate these concepts; instead, it urges a deeper exploration of acknowledged potentialities.

When a reader revels in the glory of a once-great Emperor who united the vast expanse of India and devoted the latter part of his life to imparting truthful and spiritual wisdom, the mud beneath his feet becomes almost invisible. For a Kalingan, however, it's challenging to internalize the callous proclamation of having "killed one lakh and captured one and a half lakh," as if the victims willingly exposed their necks to the sword of the ruthless Emperor.

Having such a direct connection to historical sites like Ashoka's Dhauli Edict and Hathigumpha Inscription is fascinating. Living in an area rich in historical significance evokes a more profound connection to the past. Exploring the stories of ancient times and one's ancestral roots can provide valuable insights into the region's history and culture. It is really a fascinating project. Capturing the social, cultural, and historical aspects of the Kalinga War, with emphasis on geographical features, population dynamics, religious fervour, and socio-economic conditions, adds depth and authenticity to the narrative.

A few terms of Ashoka's concept in the rock edict states:

'Avijita Kalinga' - "*Kalingyaniavijitam hi*" is found in the Thirteenth Rock Edict of Ashoka, originating from the Pali language. This certifies the cause of the conflict.

'DhammaVaye' - "*DhammaVaye*" is a term found in the Thirteenth Rock Edict of Ashoka, originating from the Pali language. It holds significant meaning, representing a deep-seated awareness and fear of religious principles or *Sanatan Dharma* in India. In various Indian languages such as Sanskrit or Odia, it retains its essence, signifying a fear of the consequences of wrongdoing in the afterlife, a concept deeply ingrained in Hinduism, Buddhism, and Jainism.

Ashoka, a man of contradictions, was a brutal leader entrusted by his father to quell rebellions in Ujjain or Takshashila, strongholds of the Maurya Dominion. However, the brutality of war at Toshali, the capital of the Kalinga Kingdom, profoundly affected him. This was a turning point in his life, a moment of realization that led to a transformation that would shape the course of history.

Furthermore the Maurya Empire operated on the principles of the *Arthashastra* of Chanakya, which extensively detailed military strategy, concepts of right and wrong, and the conduct of war and peace. Given this background, Ashoka was undoubtedly conscious of the moral complexities of warfare.

Ashoka's "*DhammaVaye*" stemmed from realizing he had not adhered to these principles during the Kalinga War. Had he fought the war with integrity and adherence to moral principles, his victory would have been celebrated triumphantly instead of tarnished by the post-war devastation of life and property.

The Kalinga War was a turning point in Ashoka's reign and spiritual journey. His sense of '*DhammaVaye*' led to a spiritual awakening, prompting him to embrace *'Dhamma Chetana,'* or consciousness of righteousness and humanity. His proclamation of *'Dhamma, Dhamma, Dhamma'* on the battlefield that he had confessed in the Rock Edicts reflects his acknowledgement of his role as an aggressor. This was a profound moment of self-realization and repentance, a moment that would shape the rest of his life and reign.

'The Atavi Land' [*"Ya pi caatavi..devanampiyasavijiteb-hoti-ta ouanunetianunijhapeti, anutape pi caprabhavedevanam-priyasa vucatitesakitiavatrapeyu, nacahamneyasu,"* i.e. Atavi... are in the dominion of the Beloved of the Gods are warned of the might of the Beloved of the Gods despite his remorse]

Warning to the Atavi people raises intriguing questions about the region's dynamics. While Ashoka's confession of guilt and remorse is clear, the warning suggests a more profound complexity in the aftermath of the Kalinga War, particularly for modern readers and intellectuals in Kalinga, known today as Odisha.

Historically, Kalinga's military strength was often associated with its aboriginal and tribal populations, who formed formidable forces such as the *Nishat* Wing led by Bhanumat, the son of King Srutayudha in Mahabharata almost one millennium ago. The Kalinga War, however, had a profound impact on these indigenous populations, altering the course of their history. Even centuries later, during the reign of Mahameghavahana Kharavela, the tribal tracts, known as the eighteen Vidyadhar states, remained crucial to Kalinga's military prowess. Additionally, these regions were renowned for their skilled archers and elephant trainers, further bolstering Kalinga's military might.

Given this historical context, the warning issued to

the Atavi people may suggest that they posed a significant threat or were feared by the victorious Emperor. The absence of mentioning the King of Kalinga in the Rock Edicts adds to the intrigue, leading some scholars to speculate that perhaps a Jain saint ruler, seeking refuge in the Atavi tract, had evaded capture during the invasion.

Historically, this is pertinent here in Kalinga and Odisha, on the event of apprehending any aggression, Lord Jagannath is hidden in some unknown tract; saving the deity is the win of the race over aggressor. So it is told once the Toshali King could outlive the war, "Our head is living, we have not lost the Kalinga War."

It suggests that Ashoka was not merely dealing with a one-sided conquest but potentially faced challenges from guerrilla warfare tactics employed by the Atavi people in the mountainous tracts. The Atavi tract was a wealthy land of diamonds and a valuable mineral reserve. However, the warning to the Atavi people adds depth to our understanding of the post-war scenario in Kalinga, highlighting the complex interplay of military strategy, resistance movements, and the enduring legacy of indigenous populations in the region.

'Second Queen Karuvaki and Prince Tivala' - Queen's Kaushambi Pillar Edict, shifted to Allahabad reads, "by the word of the Beloved of the gods, the *Mahamatras* everywhere are to be told: The Gifts here of the Second Queen, (viz.) or parks, or alms-houses, or anything else that is registered (as a gift)of the Queen, all that (are now to registered)in the manner, viz. "Of the Second Queen Karuvaki, the mother of Tivara"

It is the only archaeological finding on a Queen deeply connected with Buddhism and the Emperor's involvement.

[Buddha's mother Queen Maya Devi's dream of Airavata, the divine elephant]

Beacon:

- Rock Edicts of Ashoka, specially 13th, Kalinga Edicts, Queen's Pillar Edict
- Folktales of Odisha,
- Hathigumpha Inscription of Khandagiri and Udayagiri

Black Eagle Books

www.blackeaglebooks.org
info@blackeaglebooks.org

Black Eagle Books, an independent publisher, was founded as a nonprofit organization in April, 2019. It is our mission to connect and engage the Indian diaspora and the world at large with the best of works of world literature published on a collaborative platform, with special emphasis on foregrounding Contemporary Classics and New Writing.

Milton Keynes UK
Ingram Content Group UK Ltd.
UKHW031142121124
451094UK00006B/527